MUD, BLOOD AND MOTOCROSS

MICK WADE

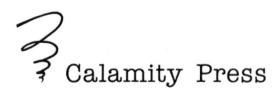

Calamity Press

This is a work of fiction. Any resemblance to events, places, names, characters or people, alive or dead, is purely coincidental.

MUD, BLOOD AND MOTOCROSS

For information visit CalamityPressInc.com.

Cover illustration and design by Mick Wade

ISBN: 978-0-9849789-0-8

To everyone out there
who has opened the throttle
and found freedom.

The 30-second board went up. Nick shifted his weight forward on the Honda CRF150. The idling motor rumbled beneath him. The roar of twenty other engines filled his ears.

He stared down the line of bikes. Billy Mackenzie looked his way and pointed at the side of his goggles. Nick nodded and steadied his gaze, looking as far down the track as he could, watching the starting gate out of the corner of his eye.

If a rider doesn't get out ahead of the pack, he'll get bogged down in a crowd of raised elbows, handlebars, and bike tires, all trying to merge into turn one. It can get ugly, but Billy had been coaching him on his start. Billy was eighteen, three years older than Nick, and a more experienced racer.

"Your reaction time is faster if you don't stare at the gate, but just keep it in your peripheral vision," Billy said.

The gate dropped, and Nick launched off the start pad. His back wheel hooked up in the dirt. It was a tangle of bikes out of the gates. Nick grabbed the next gear, shifted his weight forward on the seat, and was out in front of the pack.

Pulling the hole shot is important, but Nick knew the start wasn't everything. There were still twelve laps, 132 corners, 144 jumps, and 20 other riders to battle, not to mention the mud, ruts, whoops, and stutters—all the while trying not to crash his brains out.

Nick had a clear line ahead of him. He hit the first

—

set of jumps, gunning it up the ramp. He felt the speed and the pure thrill of flying through the air. He squeezed his knees, bracing against the seat as he landed the triple.

Less than a bike length away, Finn Foley was stalking him. Nick had seen many riders break under Finn's racing tactics. Finn's strategy was to shadow the lead rider. He would tail right at their back tire to shake the rider's concentration. He would feign a pass in one corner only to throw them off their line and sabotage their approach to a jump.

With Finn stalking them, racers would crash through the hay-bale barriers or face-plant what should have been a standard jump landing because they were thinking about Finn instead of their own lines. But Finn didn't need a big mistake to take the lead. Taking a turn too wide or easing off the throttle just a little on the straightaway would give him a chance to pass and take the lead.

Not this time, Nick thought.

Finn was sixteen, a grade ahead of Nick and Tweety, but age and size don't matter in motocross. What matters is relentless determination. Nick practiced and trained every spare second. He was hell-bent on a place in the championship, and he was not about to blow it just because Finn was lurking at his back wheel.

They were coming into the final lap. Nick stuck to his line. He could feel his heart race. *This is it.* He was going to win the first race of the season. He was going to beat Finn and Billy and Tweety. Under the faceguard of his helmet, Nick grinned.

On the straightaway he pinned the throttle, and he

knew he was pulling ahead. Nick looked back over his shoulder to see what kind of lead he had.

Five feet!

Nick turned his eyes back to the track and realized too late he was coming into turn seven too hot. He couldn't hold his line. He threw down the handlebars to make the turn.

Nick knew it was all over even before he saw Finn flash by him on the inside. Nick's back tire bogged in the rut. He yanked his handlebars and twisted the throttle. The back tire dug into the track, sending a rooster tail of dirt spraying up and out behind him. He accelerated. He tore out of the turn and hit the stutters.

He accelerated more, not letting the front of his bike dip into the ditches in between the mounds. He gained speed through turn eight and turn nine, but Finn had already pulled seconds ahead. On the final stretch of jumps Tweety was only a tire length behind him.

Once Finn had pulled ahead, it opened a hole for Tweety. Tweety managed to pull even with Nick coming out of turn ten. Just as Nick tried to make his move, Tweety passed him on the inside of the final turn.

"I stuffed you, man. I stuffed you good!" Tweety messed up Nick's hair after Nick pulled off his helmet.

"I can't believe I threw it away." Nick swatted at Tweety's hands.

"Me either!" Tweety took one more swipe at Nick's hair. "First rule of racing—never look back!"

"Bishop!" Finn shouted to Nick as he swung his leg off his green Kawasaki. "What happened? I thought you had me beat. Then you blew it."

Finn wiped the sweat from his face with the back of his hand.

"I know. I know!" Nick slumped over, shaking his head.

Nick was tired and his arms felt like noodles, but the adrenaline pumping through his veins made him want to jump back on his bike and do it again.

"Grasshopper, sometimes you have to be patient to be quicker. You have to slow down to go faster." Finn moved his lips extra after each word, imitating a dubbed kung fu movie.

"Yes, master." Nick bowed his head.

"That was fantastic, Nick. You pulled the hole shot!" Billy came up from behind and slapped Nick on the back. "Then you blew it!"

Nick shrugged. "I looked back."

Billy's race clothes were streaked with mud.

"What happened to you?" Nick asked him.

"I binned it. I got caught up at the start, so I was trying to make up time." Billy shook his head. "I pushed it too hard and went down in the ninth lap, turn five. The bike stalled out, and I couldn't get it started again."

"You're getting old." Tweety gulped down water from a sports bottle and then offered it to Billy.

"Apparently." Billy took the bottle and squeezed water over his face. He wiped the drips with his dust-covered hands, leaving muddy streaks down the sides of his cheeks and his chin.

"That's a good look for you." Kathryn Mackenzie was standing behind her older brother holding her new digital video camera. "Actually, I think it's the best you've ever looked. Maybe just a little more mud to cover up, you know, your face."

"Maybe you need a little mud on you, Kat." Billy reached out with his muddy hand toward her.

"Don't even think about it!" Kat kicked out at him, and Billy caught her sneaker midkick between his hands. Kat hopped on one leg, battling to keep her balance while trying to wiggle her captured foot free of Billy's grip.

"Be careful, you behemoth! I'm injured," Kat said waving the plaster cast on her right arm. Her broken wrist was the reason she wasn't racing today.

"Yeah, right. I forgot. You're a delicate flower." Billy lifted her foot higher.

Nick had watched variations of this scene a million times. He grew up with the Mackenzies practically next door. Billy and Kat made fighting, wrestling, and teasing a full-time occupation, and they were at it more than usual, because Billy was off to the University of Denver in the fall.

Knowing that life is going to change forever makes some people try really hard to hold on to how things are. Other times, life changes without any warning. Nick's mom popped into his head, but he pushed the thought from his mind and focused on Kat shaking her sneaker loose from Billy's hold.

Billy looked past Kat and dropped her foot. Nick, Finn, Tweety, and Kat followed Billy's gaze to a girl at the edge of the crowd. She tossed her long blond hair over her shoulder and waved at him.

"Excuse me, ladies. Gotta go." Billy wiped a streak of dirt along Kat's cheek as he walked away, but he never took his eyes off the blonde.

"Who is that?" Tweety asked.

"He said he met some girl named Jordan. That must be her." Kat wiped the dirt off her face with the back of her hand.

Girls loved Billy. When Billy walked down the halls of West Central High School, there were always two or three clinging to him at a time. He had to peel them off when he got to class.

Lucky bastard, Nick thought.

Nick tried not to make comparisons, but sometimes they were hard to avoid. Billy was tall and athletic, and all the girls at their school went gaga over his blue eyes, blond hair, and big smile. Nick, on the other hand, still had some growing to do and was definitely on the skinny side. And there was nothing, so far, about his shaggy dark hair and dark brown eyes that anybody went gaga over.

"Come on." Finn batted Nick upside the head. "Trophies."

Nick and Kat followed Finn and Tweety through the crowd up to the makeshift podium. The racetrack was basically a dirt track laid out in the middle of a field, with a hard-pack dirt parking lot and a small cement-block building with basic locker rooms, showers, and toilets. Families of the racers came with trailers and pickup trucks loaded with dirt bikes, coolers, and camping chairs, so their kids could do the one thing they loved the most: race motocross.

It was an all-day event from eight in the morning to four o'clock in the afternoon, with six to ten classes encompassing different age groups for both boys and girls. Every race kicked up more and more dust from the track, and by the end of the day, everything and everybody was covered in a thin film of gritty dust.

The race organizers presented the younger kids and smaller bike classes first. Marty Fletcher, a six-year-old who won the first moto of the day, the 65cc class, took his first-place trophy, which was almost as tall as he was. Nick knew him. He was a goofy little kid who, once he started running at the mouth, never shut up. The sun shone off his messy brown hair as he climbed down from the platform. His mom was directing him to smile and wave as she filmed him walking back into the crowd.

"Hi, Mrs. Fletcher," Tweety said in a sweet, singsong voice.

The woman's face blanched white, but she smiled weakly and backed away.

"Tweety! I won a trophy! Did you see me ride? I saw you...." Marty was still talking over his shoulder as his mom swiftly ushered him into the crowd.

"Who's that?" Finn elbowed Tweety.

"Ah, the infamous Mrs. Fletcher. She goes to my church. She was my Sunday school teacher for about a week before she quit." Tweety threw his shoulders back. "She had all five of my brothers before me, and she said I was worse than all of them put together."

"Nice." Finn nodded his approval.

"As in all things, it takes both natural talent and hard work," Tweety said.

Tweety was often misunderstood. Even when he was being sincere, his tone sounded sarcastic. He couldn't help it. His bright yellow curls looked a lot like a clown's wig, which reinforced the impression he was always joking. So if they didn't know him, people presumed Tweety was making fun of them. This got him into trouble with girls, teachers, parents, and principals his whole life. He was finally starting to accept and embrace it.

Finally, the 150cc class was called, and Finn, Tweety, and Nick climbed onto the platform as their names and race numbers were called. They jostled one another and took hold of their trophies. Nick smiled down at Kat, who was recording them again. He waved at the camera.

The afternoon had finally started to cool off. Small cotton-ball puffs of clouds dotted the deep blue sky. A little girl zigzagged through the crowd and pushed past Kat, followed closely by a boy her age. Her delighted squeal rose above the general hum.

Kat's silky black hair framed her dark eyes. Kat was beautiful. Nick wasn't the only one who thought so. She probably would have had a boyfriend the second she walked through the doors of West Central High, if she was allowed to date. It was her parents' rule, but Billy went one step farther to enforce it. He put the word out that his little sister was off-limits to anyone who valued his life.

"Don't even look at her," he had said.

Kat didn't know about Billy's intervention. She had no idea why most guys at West Central avoided eye contact with her. If she had known, she would have been furious. But no way was Nick going to tell her. He didn't want her dating some random loser any more than Billy did.

Today, she stood in the late afternoon sun, casual and confident, her hip pushed out to one side. She was wearing red shorts, and a white T-shirt that read IT'S OKAY PLUTO, I'M NOT A PLANET EITHER.

Kat recorded them on the podium and watched them on the small screen of her camera. Then she jerked her head up to watch as Nick felt a cold spray of liquid hit his face. Tweety unleashed soda from a shaken-up bottle all over Nick and Finn.

Tweety leapt from the platform squealing with laughter, and Finn tore off after him. Soda dripped down Nick's nose, and he licked his lips.

Cherry cola.

Kat tracked them with her camera, recording all the action. Finn wrestled the soda bottle away from Tweety and held him down while he poured what was left over his frizzy yellow hair. They came back over, pushing each other back and forth as they weaved through the crowd.

"Gee, so sensitive," Tweety said.

It was almost five o'clock, but the summer sun was still high above the trees. A light breeze blew through Nick's sweat-soaked hair, cooling him off and filling his nostrils with the smell of Colorado blue spruce. The breeze passed, and dust settled around the track. He wiped the cherry cola and gritty dirt off his face with his sleeve and scanned the crowd for Billy.

When they were younger, Kat and Billy's dad had brought Nick to the races every weekend, and Tweety's parents had brought Finn. As soon as Billy could drive, they had all started leaving their parents at home. So he was their ride.

Hopefully, he hasn't run off with the blonde.

But pretty girl or not, Billy wasn't the irresponsible type. He looked out for Nick, especially after the divorce. Billy had even eased Nick into high school. Being taken under the wing of a popular senior like Billy had made Nick's life a whole lot easier than it would have been otherwise.

As Nick looked around, scanning the crowd, he recognized most of the faces. The motocross race circuit was a close-knit community. Most kids had been racing since they were six or seven years old. The parents, instead of being football dads and soccer moms, were MX parents. Families shared trailers and sometimes bikes to save money. When bikes broke, families swap spark plugs or filters to help one another out. There was a spirit of cooperation in the pits, despite the competition on the track.

A man with a shaved head and wrap around sun glasses passed Nick, pushing his daughter's Yamaha YZ85 through the crowd.

"Nice start today, Nick. Keep your head in the game and this could be your season," the man said.

"Thanks, Mr. Peterson. I'm working on it."

"Say hi to your dad for me."

"Okay. See ya." Nick turned away toward the parking lot, still scanning the crowd.

Some kids would continue racing motocross, get sponsors, and eventually secure pro rides. Every ten-year-old dreamed of being the next Bubba Stewart, Jeremy McGrath or Ricky Carmichael. Even before school ended, Nick was eating and drinking motocross. He was researching techniques, training, lifting weights, and tuning his bike, anything to help him improve his lap times.

"Whoow! That's hot!" Tweety stopped in his tracks and stared past the crowd to the other side of the field at the edge of the parking lot as a female rider mounted a street bike.

Nick, Finn, and Kat peered through the crowd to look. Her bike was a new BMW GS 1200 with a custom gold paint job and white wings painted on the side of the tank. There were metallic flecks in the base paint that made the whole bike glitter in the sun. Adding to the effect, the rider was wearing skintight gold pants, a matching gold jacket, and a gold-and-white helmet. As she pulled away, doing a small burnout, Nick saw what looked like praying hands holding a rosary, circled in pinkish-gold roses, on the back of her jacket.

"Whoow. That's hot," Tweety repeated.

The smell of burned rubber drifted their way.

"She had a helmet on, Tweety. You don't know what she looked like," Nick said, turning away.

"Yeah, she's probably ugly," Finn said dismissively, all the while never taking his eyes from the golden rider vanishing into the distance.

"An ugly girl would not wear an outfit like that. Or ride a bike like that. It goes against the laws of physics," Tweety said.

"Oh, yeah? You're an expert on women now?" Nick shook his head.

"I did take Ellen Hughes to the freshman spring formal." Tweety spread his arms wide. The raising and lowering of his eyebrows implied his meaning.

"Ellen Hughes told me you stepped on her feet all night and sweat through your shirt before you finally got up the nerve to kiss her when the dance was over." Kat smirked and turned her camera on Tweety, who blushed a deep red.

He snorted and rolled his eyes.

"And she told me," Kat continued in a slightly singsong tone, "that midkiss your mom came to pick you guys up and laid on the horn like a crazy woman."

Tweety was now an even deeper shade of red, and Nick and Finn were laughing and shoving Tweety back and forth between them.

"She tried to describe the color red you turned, but I don't think she came close to doing it justice."

"My mom is a crazy woman. In the car, she gave us the infamous sex talk my brothers warned me about." Tweety shook his head.

"I'm traumatized, seriously—full-on PTSD."

Tweety always came clean, even if it was embarrassing. Actually, sometimes it seemed like he reveled in embarrassing moments. Nick was now weak with laughter. Finn was shaking without any sound escaping, until he inhaled deeply and recovered, balancing himself with a hand against Tweety.

"Come on. Let's get the bikes loaded up and find Billy, so we can get something to eat. I'm starving!" Kat said.

She turned her camera on Nick.

"So, pretty close today. Too bad you blew it."

She smiled, which softened the jab.

"In a couple weeks, when my arm is healed up, I'll show you how it's done."

"I really am sorry about your arm," Nick said.

"Yeah, well, next time, I'll know better than to give you an inch."

"You'll run me off the track next time?"

Kat smirked. "You know it."

The boys gathered up their gear and rolled their bikes through the families and spectators with their folding camping chairs and around the younger riders, who were running in circles, chasing one another, screeching, playing some unorganized game of tag. They headed to the edge of the grounds, where Billy had parked the truck and trailer.

Kat made it through the crowd headed for the parking lot faster than the boys because she was not maneuvering a bike, so it was her screams that echoed through the air a few moments later. It was Kat's ragged, panicked shrieks that made everyone stand still simultaneously, heads turned, moving as if one, toward the direction of the parking lot. Nick dropped his bike and his gear, and ran through the crowd toward Kat.

Nick ran to Kat's side and instinctively spun her around to break her gaze. He grabbed her by the shoulders and said a little louder than he meant to, "Kat! Stop screaming!"

She closed her lips tightly and blinked at him. "Was that me screaming?"

Nick nodded, but he had no idea what to do or say next. Kat swallowed hard and grabbed two fistfuls of loose fabric from the front of Nick's race jersey before glancing back at the trailer. "Do you think she's dead?"

The trailer door was open and the floor of the trailer was smooth and slick, coated with dark red liquid. *Blood*, Nick realized. Blood dripped off the edge of the trailer and ran in three separate tiny streams over the bumper. The drips were audible, forming a sickly pool in the dirt.

Lying on the trailer floor next to Billy's XR125, in the center of the red slick, was a young woman staring vacantly back out at them. Her white face was in severe contrast to the dark liquid it was partially immersed in. Her smooth blond hair fanned from her head, and at first glance appeared to be cut short. Then, with a gut-turning realization, Nick saw that her hair was long but most of the length was drenched in blood, and disappeared, camouflaged, into the red pool covering the floor.

It's Jordan.

Nick scanned the gathering crowd.

Where is Billy? What happened?

When the police arrived, Nick, Kat, Finn, Tweety, and thirty or so other people stood around waiting and watching. Nick squinted into the sun as it sank lower in the sky. He punched the redial button and called Billy's phone for the fifth time.

Still no answer.

Nick watched the officers get out of their cars. The police started questioning the adults first, but they were pointed over to where the teenagers stood. A short, stocky police officer shifted his belted holster with a tug and strode toward them, keeping his eyes on Kat, and stopped about ten feet away.

"Oh no. It's Tucker," Kat groaned under her breath.

Billy, Nick, and Kat had had a run-in with Officer Tucker a couple years ago. Officer Tucker had acted like riding dirt bikes in the abandoned quarry was a matter of national security. When Billy had pointed out that they weren't hurting anything ("How could we hurt a pile of rocks?"), Nick thought Tucker was going to lose it.

In the end, Tucker got a call on his radio and let them go. But after that, he hated Billy, and found any reason to pull him over and give him a hard time. ("Son, do you know your taillight is out?" and "You do know it's illegal to have anything hanging from your rearview mirror?") And Billy gave it right back to him. ("I see why, officer—I can barely see around this pine-scented air freshener! What a hazard! Thanks for stopping me. Thanks for the ticket! You're a real credit to your profession.")

"Young lady, step forward."

Kat looked at the cop and then at Nick, and then back at the cop. She took a tentative step forward. Tucker motioned impatiently, pointing to the ground in front of him.

"Here. Come here." His command sounded like he was talking to a disobedient dog.

Nick, Finn, and Tweety all took a step forward, in an instinctive, protective motion.

"Step back, boys. I will have questions for you soon enough."

He turned back to Kat.

"I am Officer Tucker. What's your name?"

Tucker had a pen and pad out, and he flared his nostrils over his bristly dark brown mustache while he waited for Kat to answer.

"Kathryn Mackenzie."

"Ah yes, you were with your brother, trespassing and vandalizing."

"We didn't vandalize anything!"

"Young lady, I need you to stay calm and answer my questions," Tucker barked at her.

Why do cops act like this? Nick thought. *Their moto is "Protect and serve," but in real life they hassle and condescend. As if Kat isn't upset enough by finding a dead girl, Tucker is acting like Kat is somehow responsible.*

Kat gave Nick a wary look, and he nodded at her in what he hoped was an encouraging way. Nick and the other boys watched intently, straining to hear what Tucker was saying. The cop kept his voice very low, but Nick could make out some of the conversation.

"Young lady, I am asking who the truck and

trailer are registered to."

"I'm not sure. I mean, it's our family's, but I don't know. It could be registered to my dad or my brother. Why does that matter?"

"Where is your father?"

"He's a reservist, stationed in Afghanistan."

"And where is your brother?"

Kat shook her head and looked around for Billy.

"I…ah…he should be around here."

"When is the last time you saw your brother?"

"I…I'm not sure. I…"

"What time did you discover the body?"

"I don't know. What time is it now? Maybe twenty minutes ago…"

"Have you ever seen this young lady before?"

"Yes. Earlier. I think her name is Jordan."

The cop was firing questions at Kat, asking one question almost before she had finished answering the previous one.

"Found a wallet!" a heavyset cop shouted. "New Mexico license says she's Jordan Graham, nineteen years old."

"What about your brother? Did he know Jordan?"

"Yes, I think so. They were talking."

The wind whistled through the blue spruce. Nick felt a chill run down his spine as he strained to listen.

"So what you are saying is that your brother was with this woman before she died, and now she is dead in his trailer?" Tucker's voice was full of contempt.

Kat's eyes opened wide and she staggered back a step. She shot a panicked look over to where Nick and the guys were standing. She reached out to the police officer's arm.

"There is no way Billy did this! That's not what you're saying, is it? He wouldn't hurt... He's never... There is just no possible..."

"Young lady, remove your hand, if you know what's good for you," Officer Tucker said.

Kat stepped back again. Nick grabbed her arm. She was trembling and shaking her head back and forth. Nick put his other arm at her back to steady her.

"I do not recommend you lie to me, missy."

The cop did not see, the way Nick could, that Kat was not answering one of his questions, she was trying to make this whole nightmare stop, go away, not be real.

Nick saw Billy pushing his way through the crowd.

"Billy!" Kat lurched toward her brother, but a red-haired cop restrained her.

"What happened? Somebody said..." Billy stopped and stared at the back of the bloody trailer. His face went white.

Officer Tucker stepped in front of him with a fat-fingered hand on Billy's chest.

"Mr. Mackenzie, I am going to need you to go with Officer Tenley to answer some questions."

"What?" Billy looked dazed. He was no longer in his racing gear. He was in a fresh set of street clothes—tan board shorts and sneakers—and his wet hair was leaving water drops on his T-shirt.

"Son, I suggest you cooperate." Tucker nodded his head toward the heavyset cop.

"Officer Tenley will escort you to the station and collect your statement."

Tenley came over and placed a hand firmly on Billy's arm, just above the elbow. Everything was very quiet. It seemed to Nick that everyone was holding their breath.

This is crazy! There is no way this can be happening!

He felt his stomach roll. He could still hear the *drip-drip* sound of the blood running off the back of the trailer.

Tucker then nodded at the red-haired cop, who was now more holding Kat up than restraining her. She looked limp and terrified as she watched Officer Tenley put Billy in the back of a police cruiser. Loose strands of her dark hair were blowing across her face.

"Miss, no one is under arrest, we are just taking statements. Why don't you come with me, and I'll finish taking yours." The red-haired cop walked her over to the curb and set her down gently on the grass.

Nick moved toward Kat but found himself nose to nose with Officer Tucker, who was blocking his path. The older man tugged at his belt in a shrugging motion, pushing his stocky frame even closer to Nick. He exhaled through large flared nostrils, as if he were trying to expel a horrible stench.

"I'm going to need a statement from each of you. Let's get started."

The cop put a heavy hand on Nick's shoulder, turning him firmly away from where Kat was sitting.

Tucker flipped to a fresh page in his notepad. "Let's start with names."

"Nicolas Bishop."

"Finnegan Foley."

"Lewis Emmit Clark." Tweety clearly enunciated each syllable.

Finn let out a nervous laugh.

Tucker shot a hard look at Tweety. "Son, I'm not

playing games."

"Sir, that is the name my parents gave me. Blame them. I certainly do."

Tucker raised both his eyebrows.

"Everybody calls me Tweety."

"Because of your hair?" Tucker motioned to Tweety's full, bright yellow curly 'fro.

"My hair?" Tweety looked incredulous. "No, I got my nickname because of the way I ride. I fly through the air, and I always narrowly escape the jaws of death!" Tweety was being absolutely serious, which caused Finn another snort of nervous laughter.

"And his hair is that crazy yellow color," Finn added, shrugging at Tweety's shocked look. "What? We can't lie to the police!"

"Knock it off, guys." Nick was watching Officer Tucker, whose face had hardened at every word Tweety and Finn uttered. Tucker flared his nostrils and exhaled like a bull.

"Boys, there is a dead girl over there. And in all likelihood, your friend killed her. I am the one who has to tell her parents, so I don't think this is a laughing matter." Tucker paused and let his words penetrate.

"Just answer the questions," Tucker said through clenched teeth.

It all started sinking in. A sharp pressure squeezed at Nick's temples. He could feel all his weight heavy on the soles of his feet, as if the ground might swallow him up.

Nick stared past Tucker. The rest of the police and the medical examiner were swarming like bees in and around the trailer. He watched as one female officer pulled long strands of blond hair from the latch on the trailer door. She carefully placed them in clear plastic evidence bags. She sealed and marked them, holding her pen cap in her mouth as she scribbled on the labels.

Nick didn't want to imagine it, but the picture flashed in his brain. He was seeing Billy slam Jordan up against the back of the trailer, then opening the door and forcing her in.

No way. It doesn't make sense.

Nick shook his head. He had known Billy forever. Billy had taught him how to do everything from tying his shoes to riding a dirt bike, especially after his mom ran off and his dad kind of checked out mentally. Billy was like a big brother in a lot of ways. And in all the horsing around with Kat, Nick couldn't think of a single time Billy had actually hurt her. Billy had never hurt anyone.

He had become more distant the past few years; high school sports, and girls of course, had distracted him. They didn't hang out the way they used to. But Nick had never sensed in Billy any drastic change in personality. But how well could you know anyone? Nick's mother had done a 180 and left. Was Billy capable of the same? And worse?

Maybe it was an accident? Maybe she slipped and fell?

Nick didn't know what to think. His mind was swamped with questions and doubt.

The police loaded the corpse into a body bag and lifted it from the trailer onto a stretcher. Nick didn't want to see anymore. He just wanted to close his eyes and have it all go away. But he couldn't tear his eyes

22

away from the blood-drenched scene. Two men wheeled the stretcher to the ambulance. Nick wavered, his legs threatening to go out from under him.

An officer came bounding up to where Tucker was standing. "I think we found the murder weapon. It was in the garbage can over by the bathrooms."

The cop handed Tucker a plastic bag. Inside the bag was a twenty-four-inch pipe wrench. The open serrated jaws were covered in blood.

"Have you ever seen this before?"

Tucker waved the bag in the air in front of Nick and blood smeared in streaks on the inside of the clear plastic.

Nick, Finn, and Tweety exchanged looks.

"It can't be...," Finn started.

"There is no way—" But then Tweety broke off.

The sun dipped down behind the trees, leaving them standing in shadows. Small cyclones of dust and debris swirled around the parking lot. Nick felt a chill. He had beads of sweat on his forehead.

"Tucker!" Another cop emerged from Billy's trailer. "Northern Industrial tool box was open on the floor. Set of three pipe wrenches. The twenty-four-inch is missing."

"I couldn't believe it when I saw that wrench." Finn was shaking his head and pushing food around on his plate.

"I can't believe they questioned you for three hours and never contacted your parents!" Tweety's mom dropped a platter of chicken on the table and stabbed a leg with the long two-pronged kitchen utensil she wielded. She mindlessly dropped a fresh piece of chicken on everyone's plate, even though they had all eaten seconds already—everyone except Finn.

"Mom, Finn tells you every time he comes: he's a vegetarian!"

"Mmmhmm." Mrs. Clark dumped another leg on to the pile of untouched chicken parts sitting on Finn's plate. "Don't be ridiculous."

They were all sitting around the Clarks' very large kitchen table. After the police had taken their statements, Tweety's father and brother came with their pickup trucks and tie-downs to drive them and their bikes home. It was after dark. Billy's truck and trailer had been confiscated as evidence.

Outside the kitchen window darkness and stillness settled over the small backyard, obscuring the trampoline and the vehicles parked in the driveway. Tweety's mom stalked around the table scrutinizing their plates. Mrs. Clark's name was Joyette, but Nick had never seen her joyful.

Maybe she was before she had six sons.

Tweety let out a thunderous belch, and Mrs. Clark brandished her utensil at him.

"Lewis Emmit Clark! What's wrong with you?"

"I was raised by wolves."

"Growing up with *your* older brothers, I'm sure that's what it felt like." Emmit Clark entered the room and kissed his wife on the cheek. She did not lower her weapon of choice, but she did go back to the refrigerator to pull out and prepare more food. Tweety's dad slid himself into the banquette next to Finn.

"My apologies for Mrs. Clark being so on edge," Mr. Clark said in a low, practiced whisper to Finn and Nick. "This has really upset her. She thinks she can fix it by cooking for an army." Tweety was also well practiced in the low-but-clear whisper. "That's her reaction to everything. With six of us to upset her, she's spent every minute of her life force-feeding us."

"More like cutting up the meat and tossing it into the cage," Finn said.

"Totally," Tweety laughed, and dug into his fresh plate.

Finn poked at his uneaten pile of chicken parts. Mr. Clark sympathetically took Finn's plate from him and started eating it himself.

"So what did Mrs. Mackenzie say on the phone?" Nick asked Mr. Clark.

"Well, I guess Billy was already being interviewed by the time she arrived at the station." Mr. Clark took a drink from his glass. "He's eighteen, so she couldn't get him a lawyer unless he asked for one."

"And he didn't?" Nick felt the two plates of food in his stomach lurch. He wanted to go back in time and change how things happened. And he wanted to vomit.

"No."

"But they haven't…arrested him yet?" Nick swallowed the burning that clawed at the back of his throat.

Mr. Clark shook his head. "No. They can hold him for twenty-four hours before they charge him. After they arrest him, then he'll get a lawyer." Mr. Clark stopped sawing at his chicken and exchanged a worried look with his wife. Nick thought he looked very old and papery in the kitchen's overhead light.

"This is crazy! They are not going to arrest him. There is no way Billy killed anybody!" Tweety said with a full mouth.

Nick cleared his throat. "Did Mrs. Mackenzie say how Kat is doing?"

"She's really shaken up. She feels she should have gone and found Billy before she talked to the police. She thinks she's the one who got him into trouble."

"This is crazy!" Tweety repeated. "Everybody at this table knows Billy couldn't kill anybody. It was probably some escaped felon or serial killer. I mean, it's more likely that Mrs. Fletcher killed that girl than Billy!"

Mr. Clark gave Tweety a blank look.

"Sunday school teacher," Finn whispered to him. Mr. Clark rolled his eyes up at the ceiling as he remembered the woman and the unfortunate Sunday school incident.

Nick lay in bed that night, exhausted but unable to fall asleep. Every time he shut his eyes, he saw fat drips of blood falling off the bumper into the dirt, and he couldn't push the image away. He stared at the

—

poster of Bubba Stewart hanging on his wall. He tried to think about riding and racing—anything other than what he saw today. Normally, no matter what was happening in his life, Nick could think about motocross, about a previous race or what he needed to adjust on his bike, and he could drift off peacefully to sleep, dreaming of dirt jumps and passing on the inside.

Not tonight. Every time he tried to think of riding, terrible flashes from the day intruded: Jordan's blood-soaked hair, the body bag, and the bloody wrench. It was too gruesome to be real. He rolled over onto his side, trying to turn away from the images that were clinging to him.

Nick thought of Billy in an interrogation room. He thought of Kat, standing in front of him, her eyes swimming in tears, her hands shaking with disbelief and fear, and there was nothing he could do about it.

Nick remembered that the day after his mom left, his teacher still wanted him to take the math test and memorize the spelling word list. All he wanted to do was scream, "This doesn't matter! None of this matters." Instead, he had to memorize, "Insignificant: I-N-S-I-G-N-I-F-I-C-A-N-T," and he would always remember how to spell that word.

Even tonight, when he got home and told his father what had happened, his dad seemed oblivious.

"The police will find out what really happened. You just need to trust the system," he had said.

But Nick had a terrible feeling in his stomach, because officer Tucker was the system, and it seemed to Nick like Tucker had already made up his mind.

SUNDAY

Nick woke up the next morning to the sound of squealing tires. He sat up and grabbed his jeans off the back of his chair. The tires squealed again, only louder. He fumbled in his right pocket and finally pulled out his cell phone. It was the ringtone he had picked out for Tweety.

"Yeah?" Nick rubbed his eyes, which felt gritty and rough.

"They arrested Billy." Tweety's voice was clear but there was noise, maybe a TV, in the background. "They are holding him with no bail. His mom got him a lawyer, and the lawyer wants to talk to us."

Nick struggled to clear his head.

Was this a dream?

Had he not fully awoken from some sort of bizarre nightmare? Then he remembered. All the cloying bloody images flooded back into his head.

"When?" Nick asked.

"Ten o'clock."

"Okay. I'll ride over to your house and go with you."

"Okay, so is Finn. See you when you get here."

Nick closed his phone and fell back on to his pillow.

No. Not a dream.

Nick's mom had called West Central "a pit abandoned by God and money." She wasn't exactly wrong. The Interstate bypassed the old mining town, leaving it cut off and inconvenient. West Central was in the sticks, and almost everybody's parents had to drive to the next county for work or even to go to a real grocery store or a mall. It wasn't close to any of the ski resorts, so the tourists and developers stayed away. But Nick had always seen this place as a kind of paradise.

There were hundreds of miles of trails behind Nick's house. Networks of old logging roads crisscrossed through 131 acres to the north. Those dirt roads led to the infamous abandoned quarry, where they all practiced hill climbs in piles of gravel, raced one another on the changing surfaces of stone and dirt, built jumps, and rode trails all summer long. It was freedom.

Nick put on his chest protector, elbow pads, and knee pads over his clothes. He fastened his helmet strap and adjusted his goggles. Nick jump-started his bike and entered the trail that led to Tweety's house. He sped along at a nice clip and jumped every bump and tree root.

Riding always helped Nick think more clearly. Even a trail like this one, which he had ridden a hundred times, took physical exertion and concentration. The effort always worked to clear his head. The worry and the nausea, which had weighed on Nick since Kat's first scream yesterday afternoon, evaporated. All he could feel was the power and speed of the bike and the twists and turns in the trail.

One part of the trail was so narrow that the first time he and Tweety rode it, Nick had wondered if his handle bars would even fit through the rows of trees. He shifted down into first gear. Then he picked his way through by pulling in the clutch, letting it out, easing on the throttle.

Little by little, he made it through the trail. He tried to keep his feet up on the pegs, but a few times he lost his balance and had to put a foot down to steady the bike. Then the woods opened up onto a dirt logging road, and Nick took off at full speed.

Nick accelerated and shifted up through the gears. He had the throttle pinned all the way—the bike was full whack. The speed felt so good. The wind was blowing through his shirt. The sky was clear blue above him, the fresh smell of cedars rushed into his nose, and Nick wished the road and the ride would go on forever.

Mrs. Clark was pacing back and forth behind the chairs where the boys were sitting. They had come fifteen minutes early, and the lawyer's secretary informed them that Mr. Kratchner was running twenty minutes late. "Stop fidgeting!" Mrs. Clark pointed her index finger and buried it deep in the thick volume of Tweety's bright yellow curls.

"Mom, I uncrossed my legs! You're the one wearing a hole in the man's carpet over there."

It was true. For a half hour so far, Mrs. Clark had stalked back and forth along the back wall, opening and searching her purse, not finding anything, closing it, pacing some more, and then doing the whole purse search again from the beginning. She had been jittery the whole forty-minute drive, too, scanning the three stations on the radio, clicking it off, turning it on, over and over again. The boys had been silent, a knowing look exchanged between them only once.

"Hmm. You boys hungry?" Mrs. Clark didn't wait for an answer. She threw open the door from the waiting room to the small hallway of the office building.

"Maybe there's a vending machine."

She marched out.

Even the receptionist seemed to relax after the door had closed shut behind Mrs. Clark. She slumped with relief, and then rolled her narrow shoulders like she was trying to work out some muscle tension. She tucked a fallen piece of hair behind her ear and gave Nick a relieved smile.

"Your mom is really on edge," Finn said, also finally relaxing in his chair.

"Yeah, what can I say? She can be a real freak."

The door slammed open and a very heavy man filled the doorway.

"A little help?" The man was sucking in sharp breaths, and Nick thought maybe he was stumbling in and having a heart attack. Nick grabbed his phone to call 911. The receptionist rushed forward, holding out her arms.

"Thank you, Melissa. That flight of stairs is going to kill me one of these days." The man's shirt came partially untucked as he handed the receptionist his briefcase and a tall, messy stack of files and papers. Watching the man take deep breaths and lean against the doorframe, Nick put his phone away.

He looks like a sick rhinoceros.

Melissa was a tiny woman, maybe a third of the

man's girth, and she wavered under the weight of what looked like thirty or forty pounds of paperwork. She teetered and weaved, but she finally crossed the room and placed the large pile on the desk in the office and set the bulging briefcase on the floor.

The man looked up and noticed Nick, Finn, and Tweety staring at him. "Ah. Hello. You gentlemen must be William Mackenzie's friends and witnesses."

The boys nodded. Maybe it was because of recent events, but Nick still half expected the man to fall over dead.

"I am Mr. Kratchner, William's defense lawyer."

They followed the large man into his office and stood beside the chairs meant for clients.

"Oh, excuse the mess," Kratchner said with a wave of his hand. "It's always like this."

Kratchner shuffled sideways, maneuvering his girth between the front of the desk and the chair. He scooped up the armload of papers off the seat and placed them on the already large messy pile on his desktop. The whole stack threatened to avalanche, so Kratchner kept his hand on top of the mound while he shuffled back around to his side of the desk.

"Please, sit down." The big man tentatively lifted his hand, testing the paper mountain's stability. Reassured after a moment of stillness, Kratchner dropped his substantial heft back into his chair. The leather seat groaned under its burden.

None of the boys moved. They stared at Kratchner, unsure of what to say or do next. Kratchner rested his elbows on the armrests and steepled his fingers in front of him. Finally, Nick sat down in the empty chair and Tweety and Finn sat on the couch to the right.

"How is Billy?" Nick shifted in his chair and pulled from under the cushion a red metal stapler. He held it up for a moment, but because there was no empty space on the desk, he just set it on the floor.

"Billy has been arrested for second degree murder," Mr. Kratchner said in a light, airy tone.

"Billy is being held without bail, and the case against him seems very strong."

Kratchner sighed, exhaling deeply from his nostrils.

"Most people in these situations go into denial. They hold out hope that their troubles will just magically disappear. I have a hard time convincing most of my clients how serious their situations are. Not so with Mr. Mackenzie. He seems to fully grasp that he could be facing the rest of his life in prison," Kratchner said plainly. He laced his fingers and leaned forward. "Unless you can tell me something that will prove William was in the locker room showering, like he says he was, at the time Miss Graham met her end."

Kratchner looked at each of the boys.

"Can any of you provide that testimony?"

Nick looked over at Tweety and Finn. They were both looking down and shaking their heads. Nick looked at Kratchner and shook his head as well.

Finn shrugged. "We were at the awards ceremony."

"The podium is on the opposite side of the field," Nick added.

"This is crazy! Billy didn't kill anybody!" Tweety stood, and Nick got the feeling Tweety wanted to swat at the heap of paper in frustration.

"What else can we do? What about other witnesses? There were tons of people there." Nick leaned forward.

Kratchner pulled a manila folder from the stack and opened it. "Well, according to what the police have compiled so far, there were approximately 350 people at the motocross track yesterday. They spoke to those in the immediate vicinity, about fifty total, none of whom had seen Billy in the locker room. Like you gentlemen, most of the witness statements place the crowd on the far side of the field facing the opposite direction from the trailer, and occupied by the activities at the podium at the time of the murder."

Kratchner closed the file and sank back in his chair.

"Eyewitnesses may be hard to find. But to be honest, the police are not looking very hard to confirm Billy's alibi. They have strong evidence thus far that he's guilty, and it might be enough to convict."

"What evidence?" Finn demanded.

The fat man shifted his weight in his seat, leaning one elbow on his paper-strewn desk.

"His girlfriend … dead in his trailer …killed with his wrench. It plays out as a crime of passion, a lovers' quarrel gone wrong. That's pretty convincing."

"Even if he's innocent?" Tweety threw up his hands.

"To the police he does not appear innocent." Mr. Kratchner spoke carefully in an attempt to calm Tweety down. "They have a set of facts and circumstances that point to William being responsible for the girl's death."

"They're wrong," Tweety shot back.

"What if we find someone who saw Billy in the locker room?" Nick asked.

"That would be very helpful." Kratchner smoothed down the front of his wrinkled button-down shirt.

"But you think Billy is guilty?" Nick examined the attorney.

Kratchner had dark olive skin and deep purple circles under his eyes. He looked unhealthy and tired.

"I have been at this a long time. Most of my clients are guilty. All of them claim they are innocent."

Kratchner jerked his head up as the door swung open.

Mrs. Clark burst through with an armful of snacks. The search for a vending machine was a success.

"I'm sorry, ma'am," Mr. Kratchner said as he stood up, extending his arm to signal her to stop. "I do not handle divorces."

"What?" Tweety's mother froze in confusion, the gentle sounds of crinkling snack bags whispering in her arms.

"I don't handle divorces." The ample man looked apologetic. "I'm sorry. I hate to say it, but murders and thieves are just easier to deal with."

"So it's up to us. We just need to find someone who saw Billy in the locker room from 2:35 to 3:20. That's our mission," Nick said.

Finn grabbed another bag of chips from the pile.

"Yeah, I don't think that lawyer is going to do much legwork. If he ran down leads, he wouldn't be so fat." Tweety opened another snack packet and examined its contents.

They were all at the Clark's kitchen table again, with Mrs. Clark's vending machine bounty spread out before them. Finn tore open his fifth bag of chips and greedily stuffed a handful in his mouth. He half closed his eyes and made actual moaning sounds as he chewed.

"You have an unnatural relationship with potato chips." Tweety raised his eyebrows and stared at Finn. Nick was also staring; both boys had their heads tilted to one side, frozen in almost identical positions.

"You know I don't get this stuff at home. My grandfather is a health food nut. I never get this stuff. Plus, I haven't had any real food since he became a full-fledged vegan."

Finn eyed the remaining chips, but the other two boys were still watching him intently.

"No cheese. No eggs. No milk," he explained. "And definitely no junk food."

"What do you eat?" Nick leaned forward with real concern on his face.

"Silken tofu for breakfast, instead of eggs."

"Really?" Tweety's jaw dropped.

"Fermented pumpkin seeds as a substitute for cheese."

"No way!" Nick cracked a smile.

"Mung bean salad."

"You're making this up." Tweety laughed.

Finn shook his head. "I couldn't make this up if I tried."

"I knew you were a vegetarian, but that's disgusting!" Tweety rolled off his chair, laughing.

"Do you want me to call Child Services for you?" Nick asked.

Finn stuffed another handful of chips into his mouth, shaking his head. "I'll live."

They were all laughing now.

Kat walked into the kitchen. Her face darkened, and she stared at the three of them at the table. Their laughter died abruptly, and they all looked down at their hands.

Nick searched for something to say. They were all worried. They weren't here laughing it up, forgetting that Billy was in a jail cell. Nick stood up and walked over to her. Her expression was worse than anger. She looked hurt.

"Are you all right?" Nick stood next to her. He began to reach up to touch her arm, but she jerked away and threw her shoulders back. She narrowed her eyes at him.

"I thought you cared about Billy."

She glared at him as she spoke in a small reedy voice.

"I thought you would be as worried. . . ." She shut her eyes and held back a sob.

When she opened her eyes, tears threatened to spill over her lower lashes, but Nick could see she had hardened herself. She raised her voice with every syllable.

"But no! You guys can't take anything seriously. Everything is a joke to you! You can just sit here and—"

"Kat!" Tweety interrupted. "We're ready to do whatever it takes to help Billy."

Tweety, for once in his life, said the right thing, Nick thought.

"Yeah, Kat, we were just blowing off some steam, waiting for you," Finn added. "Nick has it all worked out."

Nick whipped his head around to Finn, and Finn gave him a tiny shrug in return.

Great. What's my plan? Nick wracked his brain.

Kat eyed the three of them for a moment. Then she relaxed her shoulders. Her T-shirt pictured a rock, a sheet of paper, and a pair of scissors on the front and read CHOOSE WISELY.

She nodded and slid into a chair at the table.

"Okay. What's the plan?" she asked.

Nick felt the pressure and expectancy of all eyes focused on him. He did not have anything thought out, but the look on Kat's face made it impossible to admit that out loud. He took a deep breath to stall a minute and collect his thoughts.

"Well, to start, we'll need a full list of witnesses. We need to talk to everybody who was there that day." Nick had a pen in his hand, jotting down the ideas as they came to him. He tried to keep the panic in his gut from rising to his face. Any and all fear was best kept deep down—away from the surface.

"We need to come up with an alternative suspect. Billy didn't kill Jordan, so who did? We need to talk to her friends, family, and coworkers."

Nick started dolling out assignments.

"Tweety, get a list from the race organizers of all the racers on Saturday. We had to sign in at registration that morning, so try to get copies of those sign-in sheets. The AMA should have corresponding information, with phone numbers and addresses. You and Finn find out who was racing, and from there we'll find out who was there watching. We'll talk to all of them."

"Right, because most likely the spectators are the riders' families," Kat said.

Nick nodded. "Exactly."

"What do we ask them?" Finn emptied the last crumbs of potato chips into the palm of his hand and tossed them into his mouth.

Like Nick knew. Heat flashed in his cheeks and he cleared his throat.

"Um . . .we'll ask them if they saw Billy in the

locker room . . . or if they saw Jordan in the parking lot by the trailer." Nick scribbled down the questions on the paper in front of him while he searched his brain for other ideas.

"They have visiting hours on Mondays," Kat said awkwardly.

They all looked down at their hands, uncomfortable with the idea of Billy being locked up. They didn't know what to say. Kat sighed.

"My point is, Mom and I are going to see Billy tomorrow morning. Do you want to come with us?" she asked Nick. "He could probably tell us something more about Jordan, or maybe someone he passed on his way in or out of the locker rooms?"

"Exactly! That was exactly what I was going to say next," Nick lied.

Kat began to smile. He could see the hope spread across her face.

Unfortunately, Kratchner's words echoed in his head. As Nick was leaving the lawyer's office, the fat man had pulled Nick aside and said, "If you and your friends go digging around, you need to be prepared for the possibility that you may find beyond a doubt that your friend is guilty."

Those words haunted Nick as he laid out their plan to dig and find the truth, even if it proved that Billy did kill Jordan, even if it crushed Kat to dust. Was he really prepared for that?

MONDAY

The sky was a dull whitish-gray as Mrs. Mackenzie drove Nick and Kat to the county jail for visitors' hours. The air was hot and damp like it might rain. They all sat in the front on the bench seat of the Mackenzies' beat-up old station wagon. No one said anything. They drove south along Route 28 toward the prison, with the road humming beneath them. They each stared out into the bleak afternoon.

The car was filled with the smell of Armor All polish; the scent was a peculiar mix of fruit and grease. Nausea washed over Nick, and hot stomach acid ebbed at the back of his throat. He wiped his sweaty palms on his pants as the gray cement-block government building came into view.

It was hard for Nick to watch Mrs. Mackenzie and Kat when they first arrived in the visiting area. Only aluminum picnic tables populated the yellow room. They were in neat rows of three, spaced ten feet apart and bolted to the floor. As they waited, Mrs. Mackenzie would choke back a sob and then struggle to regain her composure, hiccuping a little with the effort. Nick hated feeling useless—powerless to help or change anything.

When Billy arrived, escorted by the guard with his hands cuffed in front of him, Mrs. Mackenzie lost her grip on her emotions and broke down in tears. The guard removed the cuffs and Billy sat down at the table and took hold of his mother's hands.

"Mom, it's okay. Please, Mom, don't cry. I'm fine. Everything is going to be okay." He looked pained as he watched his sobbing mother. The last of the color drained from Billy's face and a sheen of sweat broke out across his white forehead. Nick could see that Billy felt even more helpless than Nick did to make it any better.

"I'm sorry," Mrs. Mackenzie sniffed. "I just need a minute. I just . . ." She took a deep breath. "I spoke with your father, but he can't come home. He can't get leave. He . . ."

She squeezed Billy's hands in her own, and then she grabbed up her things and abruptly left the table. The guard on the far side of the room opened the gate for her, and she ran out.

Billy stared after her for a minute and then slumped down in his chair. Nick didn't want to look at anyone. He tried to identify what smell was assaulting him—squeezing his head behind his eyeballs.

Bleach and misery, he figured.

"This is all too much for her. She just doesn't know what to do with herself. It would be different if Dad were here, but . . ."

Kat didn't finish her sentence.

"Are you okay? Do you need anything?" she asked Billy.

Billy shook his head. He looked sickly in the prison-issue orange jumpsuit. He ran his hand over the top of his head several times while he stared at the tiny grooves on the top of the table. His short blond hair remained upright from the repetition of the motion.

The three of them sat silently, bogged down in the heavy moment. Nick knew what it was like to have a mother who walked away, who comforted herself instead of her kid. There is no other aloneness quite like it. Nick was struck dumb watching it happen to Billy.

"I'm going to go check on her." Kat rose, but Nick could see she didn't want to leave. "You're not going to be in here long. We are doing everything we can to get you out of here."

The gate clinked behind her, and Nick was struck by how many times he had heard that noise on TV and in the movies. But that in real life, that sound was so final, more terrifying than he ever could have imagined.

"Tell me everything you told the police," Nick said.

He listened intently as Billy walked him through everything that had happened after the race ended, minute by minute.

"You saw me go over and talk to Jordan. She was always joking around. She used to call me Captain America."

Nick raised an eyebrow.

"Blond hair. Blue eyes." Billy shrugged. "Wholesome. All-American. Apple pie."

"Your red-white-and-blue race gear," Nick supplied.

Billy tried to smile, but it looked more like a pained grimace.

"She asked me if I wanted to hang out later. I said yes, I just had to drop you guys and the bikes off first. We were going to meet at her place at six." His voice was flat and monotone. Billy rattled off the facts, which Nick realized he must have repeated many, many times in the last forty-eight hours.

"She walked with me over to the trailer. I rolled my bike in, strapped it down, and grabbed my bag with my towel and clean clothes from the back. I figured you guys would be there any minute and . . . I don't know, I just wasn't worried about it." Billy shook his head.

"Worried about what?" Nick asked.

"The cops kept asking me why did I leave it unlocked? Why didn't I lock it?"

Billy ran his hands over his hair again.

"But I wasn't worried about anybody stealing anything. You know how it is."

He shrugged.

"I've never had anything stolen at the track! And I certainly never thought that . . . anything like this could happen." He rested his elbows on the table and shuddered. He put his face in his hands.

Nick didn't say anything. Watching Billy was like watching Mount Everest crumble, watching a continent sink into the sea. The world would never be the same. He waited for Billy to continue.

"She teased me about my crash as I secured the tie-downs. She was saying she hoped I didn't have commitment issues. I had to commit to the turn. Commit and be fearless."

"She raced motocross too?" Nick asked.

Billy shook his head.

"No, she rode a street bike."

He looked so different to Nick. The usually happy, worry-free, carefree Billy that Nick knew had been replaced by this other person. Dark circles shadowed his eyes and the orange jumpsuit made his skin look gray.

"We said good-bye, and I went into the locker room to shower and change. I got out and the police were there. Jordan was dead. The police think I'm lying!" Billy's voice broke.

He sighed and then spoke more softly, almost a whisper.

"And now I'm here."

He shrugged again and sagged farther down in his chair.

"I really liked her. I never would have . . ." Billy choked on his words and had to clear his throat. "I would never hurt anyone."

Billy stared at the table for a while. He ran his fingers though his hair.

"You know I didn't do this? Right?"

Nick didn't know what to think. He did know in his gut that Billy couldn't murder anyone. But all the evidence pointed to Billy. Billy had been with Jordan by the trailer.

"Why would someone kill her?" Nick asked.

"I have no idea." Billy shook his head. "She seemed really smart and funny, but gutsy and tough too, like she could take care of herself, you know? But, then again, I didn't know her for very long."

Billy ran his finger along the grooves in the table.

"Jordan wasn't like anyone I ever met before. She was fun. I never knew what to expect, you know? Our first date, she took me pool hopping, but only places where the people were home. They were inside watching the eleven o'clock news, and we were swimming naked in their pool."

A smile crept across Billy's face. "She really believed that anything was possible, and she kept saying her next step was going to Ontario and becoming a singer/songwriter, and after that she would move to Africa and guide safari tours. She had all these big dreams, and she really felt like all she had to do was pick one, and she could make it happen."

"Did you ever meet her parents?"

"No way, it sounded like she didn't get along with her mom at all. Her parents dumped her at some horrendous Catholic school for troubled girls—Our Lady of Mercy. She said it was the perfect name. And she painted this picture of the nuns wrestling all these teenage girls for their immortal souls."

Billy shook his head and leaned forward with his elbows on the table.

"With Jordan everything could be fun, you know? She was never bored—anything and everything could be an adventure. Optimistic, I guess, but . . . lit from the inside. Does that make sense?"

Nick nodded.

Billy dropped his hands on the table. All the lightness and animation that he had had a minute ago fell away.

"I can't believe she's dead."

Nick watched his friend's face. Billy wasn't just scared because he was in jail; he was wrecked over loosing someone he obviously cared for. Nick leaned toward Billy and kept his voice soft.

"When did you meet her?"

"Three weeks ago, Kevin Hammel had a party. She was there."

"Kevin Hammel?" Nick raised his eyebrows.

Kevin was not someone Nick thought Billy hung out with.

"Don't look at me like that. I went with Egghead. He knows Kevin from wrestling back in the day."

Egghead was one of Tweety's older brothers. All of the Clark boys were unfortunately named, and even more unfortunately nicknamed. Jacob Emmit and Daxton Emmit, the two oldest, were called Wile E. and Bosko. Moyle Emmit went by Egghead, and Shilo Emmit and Zekiel Emmit went by Rocky and Mugsy. Tweety got off pretty good, all things considered.

"Did you meet any of Jordan's friends or did she

talk about anyone? Family?"

Billy took a deep breath and tried to remember. "She talked about her friends like they were family."

"Her friends from Our Lady of Mercy?"

"Yeah. Some, I think. Her best friend, Kayla, went to Catholic school with her. She lived with a bunch of other girls too. You could go there and talk to her roommates, the big apartment above the Red Brick Tavern."

Billy leaned back in his chair and gripped his hair as he ran his fingers through it. He made a slight grimace. "Although . . . they didn't really seem to like me all that much."

"Why?"

"I don't know. I figured it was the usual protective-best-friend stuff, but one time . . ." Billy stared off into space, remembering something.

"One time, what?" Nick tried not to raise his voice.

"It's funny. One time I overheard one of her friends talking about me, telling Jordan to be careful. Don't let it get serious. That I was a distraction."

"A distraction from what?"

"I don't know. I didn't really think about it until just now."

"Billy, think! This is important."

"You don't think I realize this is serious, Nick? I'm the one in jail!"

"Sorry." Nick sat back. "Can you think of anything else? Was she involved in anything . . . dangerous?"

"Like what?" Billy narrowed his eyes at Nick and shook his head. "She didn't deserve this."

—

48

The gate rattled open.

"Time's up." The guard came over and Billy held out his hands for the cuffs. Nick felt like punching that guard, screaming and tearing the cuffs away. It seemed unreal. Nothing this unfair could be real.

Billy paused and turned back to Nick before he went through the gates. "Tell my mom not to worry about me. And . . ." His words fell off. "Just look out for her and Kat for me. Okay?"

Nick nodded. The metal door clinked shut, and it sounded to Nick like the end of the world.

Nick sat in the empty visitors' room for a minute. He took a deep breath and dreaded the drive home.

Maybe Mrs. Mackenzie won't cry again, Nick thought hopefully.

"You staying?" a thick-necked guard asked at the other gate.

"No." Nick practically convulsed at the thought of staying.

The guard opened the gate. Nick walked out, leaving the visitors' room and walking out through a series of contained hallways. A gate would lock behind him before the gate in front of him would open.

Finally, Nick stepped out into the jail's main lobby. Nick was lost in thought, staring at the fake terrazzo floor and the bolted-down benches lining the room, when he walked smack into Officer Tucker. Nick staggered backward, but he caught his balance before he fell.

Tucker's nostrils flared, and he scowled at Nick like he was a filthy pile of garbage.

"Only an animal would do such a thing to that

poor girl."

Tucker curled his lip as he spit out the words. Nick didn't know what to say.

"Well?" he barked at Nick.

Nick was taken back by Tucker's wrath. The words hit him like a slap in the face. His heart raced. He wanted to defend his friend and tell Tucker he was wrong about Billy, but he had an irrational flash of fear that Tucker would grab him, throw him into a cell, and clink the metal gate closed behind him.

Tucker tugged at his belt, adjusting his holster. When Nick didn't respond, Tucker exhaled dismissively through his nostrils and walked past him. The *click-click* sound of his footfalls faded.

Nick was alone in the lobby, feeling both relieved and sick. He felt like a coward.

This is impossible, Nick thought. *How can this be happening?*

Back at his house, Nick added notes to the sketch of his plan. In bold letters under "Jordan" he drew out two prongs and wrote "Roommates" at the end of one and "Kevin Hammel" at the end of the other.

Kevin Hammel was a former high school wrestling star and now a small-time drug dealer. Four years ago, a few weeks after his graduation, he passed out drunk in the parking lot of Lala's Little Nugget, where he was drinking with a fake ID. He curled up on the pavement in the fetal position, and sometime later that night, Alex Perry, owner of Perry Brothers Plumbing, who was a little lit himself, backed his car over Kevin.

Aside from being paralyzed from the waist down, Kevin made a miraculous recovery. Plus, he received five hundred thousand dollars in a lawsuit settlement. Alex Perry had to sell his business and move in with his eighty-seven-year-old mother to pay Kevin the damages that weren't covered by his car insurance. And two women plumbers now owned Perry Brothers, but they hadn't changed the name.

Kevin Hammel bought a piece of property off Route 28 and built a little cabin on the side of what was arguably a large hillside. However, because Kevin had a road built up the hill to the cabin, he grandiosely named the hill Mount Hammel, and the road became Mount Hammel Road.

Kevin could see for miles in all directions from his house, so it was the perfect place to throw parties and sell drugs. Kevin could see the cops approaching from Route 28 in both directions, and any drugs or anyone under age could disappear out the back into the woods. Then Kevin would roll his wheelchair out onto the front porch and wave at the police cars at they drove up his road.

Nick figured he had to go to Kevin's at just the right time in the day.

Too early and he'll still be asleep, too late and he'll be too drunk to answer questions.

Nick looked at his watch.

Four o'clock. Might as well give it a shot.

Nick threw on his gear and left a note on the kitchen table. He rolled his bike out of the garage and shook it to make sure he had enough gas in the tank.

Should be fine.

He set off through the woods for Mount Hammel. The long shadows fell across the thin dirt trail, and thoughts flashed through Nick's brain the same way light and dark passed over his helmet. Sun. Shade. Hope. Fear.

Nick crossed over a small swift stream. A doe with her speckled fawn stood twenty feet downstream and watched Nick as he watched them. The trail rose steeply up the backside of Mount Hammel, and Nick accelerated up the incline. He hammered the throttle and felt the bike open up. Hill climbs on a powerful dirt bike were up there in the top-five best things in life.

He crested the hill and picked his way through the woods, until finally he could see the back of Kevin's cabin. Nick stopped at the edge of the woods and let the bike run idle for a minute. He waited to see the curtains draw back, and then the back door slid open.

Kevin Hammel rolled his wheelchair out onto the back deck, a compact black gun in his hand and a bottle of Wild Turkey set between his thighs. Nick took off his helmet and pressed the kill button, silencing the motor, but he stayed seated on the bike.

Best not to get shot, Nick figured.

"You lost?" Kevin drawled.

"I'm Nick Bishop. I'm a friend of Billy Mackenzie."

"Billy? Everyone's saying Billy killed some girl." Kevin rested his gun in his lap.

"I can't believe it. Is it true?" Kevin took a swig from his bottle.

"No, it's not true. That's what I came to talk to you about. Can I ask you a couple questions?"

A girl stepped out on the back porch. She was in a red tank top with thin straps and pink cotton panties.

Nick felt his face flush.

"I don't have anything better to do!" Kevin called out.

"What are you shouting for?" The girl lit a cigarette and leaned against the deck railing. She glanced at Nick but seemed unfazed by an audience.

"Why don't you come inside, little man?" Kevin swatted away the cloud of smoke that drifted from the girl's cigarette, and beckoned Nick into the house with a welcoming wave of his gun.

Nick hopped off the bike, crossed the yard, and walked up the wooden ramp that led to the deck. The girl was leaning on the railing, humming and singing to herself. She sang a few words and then hummed a few notes. Nick assumed she was filling in when she didn't know the lyrics.

Her silky dark brown hair was parted in the middle and hung down, covering most of her face.

When Nick stepped closer, he saw she had dark circles under her bloodshot eyes. Staring into space, she ignored him as he passed. She leaned farther over the railing and the back of her tank top pulled up, revealing five or six inches of skin between it and the lace edge of her underwear.

Nick stepped over the threshold into the house and gave one more glance over his shoulder at the girl's bare legs and her pink panties. There were two other girls in tank tops lying on the couch inside, although from what Nick could see they had shorts on.

There was a skinny guy with big hair sitting on the floor next to the coffee table, and a hulking, muscle-bound guy with dark hair and cargo pants in the recliner. A little beefier than your average junkie, but maybe he was still green. The coffee table had empty bottles and empty glasses covering the surface. The skinny guy cleared off a small spot and started crushing a white pill on the table with the back of a spoon.

Nick followed Kevin through the living room and into the kitchen. Every surface of the kitchen was littered with bottles, mainly Wild Turkey bourbon whiskey bottles like the one Kevin had in his lap. Kevin wheeled himself up to the open side of the table and motioned with his gun to the chair across from him.

Nick took a seat. "Do you ever put that down?"

"Which?" Kevin held up both the bottle and the gun, and then answered the question for both. "No, never."

He laughed a high-pitched, cackling kind of

laugh. He was missing several of his teeth.

"Is that what you came here to ask?"

"I'm here about that girl, Jordan."

Kevin nodded and took a drink of bourbon but didn't say anything. The bottle was half full.

Or half empty, if Kevin is a pessimist.

Nick felt hot acid flood the back of his throat. He tried not to fidget. The stench of alcohol burned as he breathed it in. The smell brought back visceral memories. Trying to wake his mother out of a stupor. Thinking she was dead. Nick shut the images out—slammed the door on them.

"Can you tell me anything about Jordan?" Nick asked.

Kevin took another swig of Wild Turkey.

"Billy said he met her here a few weeks ago," Nick prompted.

"Mmm. She was hot." Kevin's eyes were red and unfocused. "I have a hard time picturing Billy bashing her head in."

Kevin slurred the word "picturing," and Nick realized he might have come too late in the day after all.

"Billy, man, he's a lover, not a fighter, you know?" Kevin said.

"Did Jordan talk at all about friends or family? What do you know about her?"

Nick leaned forward to put his hands on the table, but there was no empty space. So he sat back in his chair.

"Where did she work?" Nick continued to prompt.

"What are you, some kind of midget cop?" Kevin sneered.

"Like I said, I'm just trying to help Billy out." Kevin shrugged, pacified.

"I don't know. She seemed the trust fund type. Nice clothes, fancy new motorcycle, lots of free time."

Kevin leaned his head from side to side, cracking his neck.

"I met her a few weeks ago at Slim's. She was there with another blond girl. They said they were sisters. Very hot, but the sister was a bitch, if you know what I mean. She didn't like my ride." Kevin spun his wheels forward, lifting the front end in the air. He slammed the small front wheels down with a bang and took another drink.

"Anyway, the dude in there with the short hair, Ben, he's the bartender there. I extended an invitation to him, and he brought the girls here with him." Kevin shrugged and looked past Nick into the living room. "But I guess Jordan liked Billy better, because that's who she left with. Ben and her sister seemed kinda pissed."

"Do you think Ben would know anything about her?" Nick twisted in his seat to look into the living room.

The girl in the pink underwear was dancing slowly in front of the recliner. Ben watched lazily as the girl pulled off her red top.

"I don't know, but I wouldn't disturb him now."

Nick watched the girl until Kevin started cackling again.

Just as Nick turned back toward Kevin, there was a loud crash. The dancing girl fell over the coffee table. She was sprawled on the floor in her pink bra and pink panties. There were bottles clattering down and clinking together on the floor around her. Bright red blood flowed down her face and chest from her bleeding nose. No one moved. She was on the floor bleeding and everybody just stared.

Kevin shouted, "Gillian, do not bleed on my carpet!"

Nick got up and wet a dish towel with cold water. He brought it over to the girl, but when he handed it to her, she just looked at it. He put it in her hand, and still she didn't do anything. Nick pushed her hand with the dish towel up to her bloody face, and then she seemed surprised to see the bright red against the grimy towel.

Nick felt sick. He felt pity for Gillian, and then he was flooded with anger.

Serves her right.

The whole scene reminded him of a horror film.

Nick left the house feeling dizzy. He hung his helmet on his arm and rolled his bike into the woods, out of sight from the house. He leaned his bike up against a tree. Slumping down to the forest floor, he braced his head in his hands.

The sharp sting of bourbon still clinging to his nostrils, he started thinking about Ace Raceways and the first time he raced there. It used to be a cow farm, but they turned it into a motocross track. It became a pretty big venue, with races on Wednesday nights and Saturday afternoons. These days, the smell of cow manure was very faint, but that first year, it was overwhelming. There were flies, too. Big fat horse flies bit Nick's flesh while he lined up for the race.

It was his first time racing in the 150cc class. He had done well on his old 80cc, and everybody thought he was ready for a bigger bike. In hindsight, Nick realized it was too much too soon—bad timing with everything else going on at home.

The new bike, new race class, and new track proved a disastrous combination. And it wasn't even the pain that bothered Nick, although there was plenty of pain; it was the humiliation. Four years later, his face still flushed with memory of it.

At the gates, he had been more nervous than ever before. Nick had been up most of the night before, listening to his parents shouting downstairs. He felt hot and queasy. The new bike felt foreign, whereas his old 80 felt like an extension of himself. The gates dropped and he took off, but then he fumbled the shifter, kicking it into neutral instead of second, slowing down just as the pack was funneling into the sweeping right-handed first turn.

Bikes collided with his. Three bikes went down, but Nick threw out his leg and managed to stay up. He kicked the bike into gear, but the back of his leg got shredded by somebody's foot peg in the mangle of interlocked bikes.

Nick pulled away, furious with himself for such a stupid mistake. It was his fault the other bikes had crashed. Nick was thinking about that as he went through the high-speed rhythm section, instead of focusing on riding, and the next second, he was flying through the air over his handlebars. Even in the few split seconds before he hit, he was cursing himself out midair. *Stupid. So stupid!*

He hit the dirt with a rib-rattling thud. He jumped up as fast as he could and dragged his bike to the side of the track. Bikes roared by him, spitting up clumps of dirt from their knobby tires. Nick tried to kick-start the bike, but after his first try, he was so light-headed, he almost fell over. He rested his head on the bars for a second. Everything seemed to go quiet.

Come on! Nick thought to himself. *Do this!* He gritted his teeth and took a deep breath. The roaring motors of the lead bikes came up behind him. He stomped on the kick-start lever - the motor rumbled. Nick took off down the straightaway, only to be passed over and over and over, through turn three, turn four, on the stutters, and through turn five.

Turn nine was a steeply cambered turn, and as number 15 passed Nick on the inside, the rear tire threw up a rooster tail that clobbered Nick in the face and chest. Each clump of dirt that smacked him stung his pride. He downshifted and tore down the straightaway after number 15. He braked late coming into the turn, lost the rear wheel, overcorrected, and high-sided again.

He landed face first in the dirt. He tried to get up, but he was winded. He stayed down on one knee, gasping for breath. He coughed and gasped some more. Sucking in the thick scent of cow shit. Wobbly on his feet, Nick staggered over to his bike. The other riders were swerving around him, creating thick clouds of shit-smelling dust on either side of him.

He swiped at his goggles, but the dirt wasn't blocking his vision as much as the stinging, burning tears. His mind was so hot, flooded with anger and frustration. He kick-started the bike and opened up the throttle. He saw Mr. Clark on the far side of the race barriers. He was motioning for Nick to pull off the track, but Nick ignored him. Nick was three laps down when the checkered flag went up. He came around the final turn and crashed once more, this time hearing a distinct "pop" from his right shoulder.

The medics at the track sorted out his dislocated shoulder and told Mrs. Clark he had a fever of 103. Nick had the flu. The worst part—being sick and crashing out and making a fool of himself and dislocating his shoulder was not the worst part. That came later, when he got home and she had packed up all her things and left, for good this time.

Nick shook his head as he remembered it all. Billy, Kat, everybody, saw him fail miserably. They all babied him for months afterward. It was humiliating and infuriating. Why was he thinking about this now? He needed to turn that off and focus on the real problem—Billy.

The sky began to darken with storm clouds. There was a cool breeze forcing the young pines to bend and sway. Nick pulled himself up off the ground. It was getting late, probably close to dinnertime, and Nick knew he should head home. He kick-started the bike and looked down the hill toward Route 28, but instead of turning around and going the way he had come, he angled his bike downhill and headed the back way to the Strip.

"The Strip" was actually just a dingy collection of four stores, two strip malls, and a gas station along the main county road. He rode out of the woods to the smaller of the two strip malls, into the parking lot behind the hair salon. He leaned his bike against the Dumpster, wishing he had brought his U-lock. He hoped for the best and walked around to the front side.

The façade of the complex was covered in pinewood siding to give it that rustic, old-fashioned, boomtown look, but it didn't change the fact that it was a sad, ugly strip mall. Touch of Class Hair Salon was busy, an old lady under every dryer getting her hair set. Nick passed the dirty windows of the Dollar Store and the Wagon Wheel Diner. He got to the final storefront and walked into Slim's Irish Pub.

Nick's eyes adjusted to the dim interior. He looked down the length of the speckled, Formica-topped bar and the row of barstools with torn and patched red vinyl seats.

A dark-haired woman emerged from the back and stalked down the bar toward him. Her arm was extended, pointing toward the door. Her jaw was set and her lips pursed into a stern pout. "You might as well turn around, kid. I don't care what your fake ID says. I am not serving you."

She was the owner, Greta Stapleton. Nick had seen her before when she brought her Ford Focus into his dad's garage. She had a deep wrinkle in the center of her forehead, and small hard wrinkles at the corners of her eyes and mouth. Nick didn't think she looked Irish or slim, and wondered for a moment how she came up with the name for the bar.

"I'm not here to drink." Nick held up his hands in surrender. "Do you know Ben?"

"Ben?" She dropped her arm. "What's he done?"

"Why do you ask that?" Nick asked. He had a strange feeling about the dark-haired druggy, which is why he had come here in the first place. He didn't seem to fit in. Not at Slim's, where most of the men looked more like alley cats than body builders, and not at Kevin Hammel's, mainly because he still had all of his teeth.

"He started working here a month ago—just moved from San Diego."

Greta wiped her hands on a towel and then tucked the end of the towel back into her apron pocket. "He's a good bartender, but he's been looking all over town for trouble. In four short weeks he's met every tramp, scumbag, and drug dealer within a fifty-mile radius. They've all started congregating here. More than usual, I mean." She shook out her dark curls behind her, obviously annoyed.

"Lucky me," she sighed, throwing out her hands.

"Do you know where he lives?"

The woman frowned. "I think he's got a room at

Lakewood. He won't be there, though. I certainly wouldn't be, if I lived in that dump." Her top lip curled at the thought. "He's always out wherever the party is, up at Kevin Hammel's probably, or over at the Breeze Inn. But I've got his cell number."

She went behind the bar and jotted Ben's number on a scrap of paper. She held the paper out, but as Nick reached for it, she pulled it back. "What do you want with Ben?" She eyed Nick suspiciously. "Are you looking for drugs?"

"No." Nick tried to think of the right angle to get Greta to talk to him. "I'm a friend of Jordan Graham."

"Oh! Sorry. I heard what happened. Ben was really upset about it." She frowned, wrinkling her whole face. Greta handed Nick the paper with a dramatic sigh. "I guess that Billy Mackenzie is a real nut case. I hear he killed that girl in a jealous rage." Her hands were on her hips, denting into the bulge of flesh hanging over her jeans.

"Who told you that?" Nick asked.

"Cops were here last night to break up a fight, and Officer Tenely filled me in." Greta took a seat on a stool at the end of the bar. As she made herself comfortable, the vinyl creaked and squeaked. "People do all kinds of crazy things you'd never expect them to, you know. Terrible things."

Greta leaned forward like she was sharing a secret with Nick. "My usual bartender, Judy, her husband worked for the same trucking company for fifteen years, and then out of the blue, he runs off and steals a whole semi full of Oxycontin. Poof! Vanished!"

She threw her arms in the air. Greta sounded delighted. She pronounced it "oxy-cotton" as if it were a laundry detergent. She spoke quickly, without seeming to take a breath once she got going. "I mean, he's probably in Guadalajara or Cabo by now. But who would have guessed? I mean, you never would have thought that Gus had it in him to do something like that. Judy thought after the fact that maybe there was another woman, but to tell you the God's honest truth, I just can't see it. Gus was no prize. He had a beer gut and bad breath. It's just terrible for poor Judy, though. She sold the house and moved in with her sister in Utah."

Greta said it was terrible, but she was smiling and seemed to be thoroughly enjoying herself. Bad news and terrible rumors traveled unusually fast in this town, and the reason was Greta. "But he could be anywhere. That Oxycontin is just all over the place. People all strung out on it—young people, old people, it doesn't matter. Officer Tenely told me he answered a call up on the north side, in the apartment complex past the car wash."

Greta lowered her voice again, as if she were confiding in Nick. "Neighbors called in a complaint about a crying baby. Well, they broke down the door and there was this young couple all strung out, while their two little babies screamed their heads off in the next room. And it was these prescription pills! I mean, honestly, I don't know what's wrong with people today."

Nick shifted his weight from one foot to the other and wondered how he was going to get out of there.

"Well, I better get going." Nick backed away toward the door. "Thanks." *Well, that was a waste of time. What was he looking for anyway?* Nick turned to go, but he spun back, finally remembering something useful. "What's Ben's last name?"

"Sherman." Greta seemed deflated that their talk was over. She exhaled a sigh and looked around the empty bar, hoping for someone else to walk in and listen to her.

"Thanks," Nick said, and hurried out into the oncoming storm. The sky was thick with dark gray clouds, and the wind was picking up. Nick ran around to the back of the building to his bike. He hoped the rain would hold off for the twenty or so minutes it would take him to ride home. He looked up at the sky and two fat raindrops hit him in the face.

No such luck.

Nick sped up the hill at a diagonal, trying to avoid pits and rocks. Lightning flashed directly behind Nick, and the clap of thunder almost startled him into crashing. At the top of Mount Hammel he turned left and headed into the woods. He followed the same trail he had taken to Kevin's earlier in the day, but now every root was slick and the trail was very quickly turning into mud. Nick came out of the woods and battled the downside trail.

The rain came down in steady sheets. He downshifted and was careful to lay off the front brake. He lightly worked the back brake when he absolutely had to, but mainly he let the gearing modulate his speed. The last thing he wanted was to go over the handlebars and land headfirst on a rock. He just wanted to get home and get dry.

He lost the back end in the mud but grabbed the clutch and threw out his right leg. He barely kept the bike from falling. Nick could feel every beat of his heart banging through his head. He took a deep breath and tried to focus.

His goggles were fogging up so he tore them off his eyes and left them propped up on his helmet over his forehead. *Damn it!* The water streamed down his back and filled up his boots. He kicked the bike into second gear and kept his eyes focused on the trail ahead of him.

Nick splashed through the rushing stream at the bottom of the hill and the bike lurched and stalled out.

Out of gas? You've got to be kidding me!

He hated it when he did stupid stuff like this. He didn't have enough gas in the tank to make the detour to the bar and play detective. He should know better. It made him furious—angry at the rain, mad at the mud, but mainly pissed at himself. Nick kicked the bike into neutral and pushed it through the mud, cursing and kicking the rest of the way home.

"What happened to you?" Randy Bishop looked up from the kitchen table to stare at his son, covered from head to toe in mud and dripping on the welcome mat.

"I went for a ride. I got caught in the rain."

"Don't move. I'll get a towel." Nick's dad jumped up from the kitchen table, and Nick heard him climb the stairs to the linen closet. Nick could feel his anger shifting toward his father.

It's not like they kept their house spotless, but Nick's dad hated messes. He preferred to avoid them rather than clean them. To that end, they only used paper cups and paper plates, if they used plates at all. Nick understood the logic, but sometimes it was ridiculous—like, what was so hard about loading the dishwasher like a normal person? It was one more thing his dad couldn't handle after Nick's mom left.

His father had streamlined their routine in a way that left their house and their lives feeling even more empty than they needed to be. Randy Bishop now only bought frozen food. Breakfast, lunch, dinner, it was all Hot Pockets and Stouffer's frozen French bread pizzas.

It wasn't like Nick's mom was ever any kind of domestic goddess. As far back as Nick could remember, his dad had done most of the cooking and cleaning. But after she left, he seemed to give up, like he was taking care of her all those years, like it was for her and not for Nick. He used to use this one brand of fabric softener sheets that smelled exactly like its name, Clean Burst. But after his mom left, his dad stopped using it, and now Nick's clothes smelled like nothing.

A few years ago, Nick had helped his dad fix an eight-cylinder van. His dad explained that you can lose compression in one cylinder and not even notice, but you lose compression in two and all of a sudden you lose a lot of power.

His dad had said, "You could still drive this van around for a while, but any minute it could break down on the side of the road."

After Nick's mom walked out on them, his dad was just like that van, running on six cylinders and in danger of breaking down. So Nick had to be careful with his dad. He feared what would happen if he wasn't.

Nick's dad came down the stairs and handed him a worn pink bath towel. "You didn't come by the garage today."

"Yeah, I went to go check on few things for Billy." Nick wiped his face and rubbed the towel over his soaking wet hair.

"You didn't call."

"I know. I'm sorry. I had a lot on my mind. This thing with Billy, you know?" Nick pulled a kitchen chair over to him and sat down while he peeled off his muddy boots.

"You know what's really crazy? This jerk, Officer Tucker, is convinced Billy is guilty, and it seems like as far as he's concerned the investigation is over. The cops don't give a damn about what really happened!"

"Nick, that's no way to talk. I know Tucker. We went to high school together. He's not a bad guy. He does everything by the book. I'm sure the police are doing everything they can to investigate what happened."

"I'm telling you they're not!" Nick was shouting.

Why is Dad acting like this is no big deal?

"Would you feel this way if it was me in jail right now?" he asked his dad.

"You are not in jail, and I would like to keep it that way. I don't want you interfering with this. Let the police and Billy's lawyer do their jobs. I know he's your friend, but there is no reason for you to be in the middle of this."

"I can't believe you are saying this. We're talking about Billy!"

"People are not always what you think they are! And people change, and sometimes they do things you never thought they could do."

Nick didn't say anything. It always came to this. No matter what they were talking about, they were always talking about her.

His dad cleared his throat and continued. "You should read this article in today's paper. And you should prepare yourself for the possibility that Billy may have hurt this girl. Maybe he didn't mean to, but . . ."

"No." Nick threw his muddy boot against the front door. Mud splattered on the red door and the white trim. "You are wrong about Billy! And you were always wrong about her. She was never perfect! She was always a drunk."

Nick stormed out of the kitchen, hating his father, his mother, Officer Tucker, and pretty much the whole rest of the world.

The moon shone in through Nick's bedroom window, a day or two from being full. Still, the light shone in on Nick like a spotlight.

What am I going to do?

But Nick had no idea. He believed Billy, but he had so many questions. The digital clock glowed a red 12:45. It had been such a long day. Nick thought about Billy in jail, Gillian bleeding on Kevin's carpet, and all the things Greta Stapleton had said.

There was no way he was going to fall asleep. Stepping over the creaky board by his dresser, he crept downstairs. The paper was still spread out to the article about Jordan's murder.

"Girl Bludgeoned at Local Sporting Event," the headline read. The article cited several recent cases of teenage girls killed by jealous or wacko-possessive boyfriends. There'd been a sharp rise in physical abuse of teenage girls by their crazy boyfriends. One girl in Texas was stabbed when she tried to break up with her boyfriend. In Maryland, a seventeen-year-old psycho stalked his girlfriend. He eventually kidnapped her, and they found her body floating in a lake.

Who were these freaks? Who acts like that?

The article went on to say that Billy and Jordan were dating, and according to the police, he "allegedly bludgeoned" her in a jealous rage. The article ended, "Jordan Graham is survived by her parents Melissa and Jonathan Graham of Phoenix, Arizona."

Well, they've all decided he's guilty, Nick thought.

TUESDAY

The next morning, Nick pulled out his notes. He wrote down "Parents in Phoenix, AZ," and wrote their names below that. He snapped open his phone and held down the number 1, speed-dialing Kat.

"Hi, any progress?" Kat said on the other end of the line.

"Not much. I was wondering if you could find a phone number?"

"Sure, for who?"

"Jordan's parents." Nick gave Kat all the information he had gotten from the paper. "Maybe you could call as a reporter and get some more information? First of all, find out if she had a sister. Kevin said he met her sister, but there was no mention of one in the paper."

"What else did Kevin say?"

"He thought she might be a trust fund kid with lots of free time, a new bike, and all that."

"Why would a rich kid choose to move to West Central and live above the Red Brick Tavern?"

"I know, it doesn't really make sense. So, if she wasn't rich, where did she work? Did her parents know any of her friends?"

"I'll see what I can do," Kat said.

"I'll call you later." Nick snapped his phone closed, and went back to his notes. Under "Kevin Hammel" he drew a line down and wrote "sister?" He drew a second line and wrote "Ben Sherman." He drew two lines down from Ben's name and wrote "Lakewood View Motel" and "Breeze Inn."

Lakewood View Motel did not have a view of a lake. The closest lake was fifty miles away. The dingy motel was built in the 1970s and had a view of Route 28. It was a stone's throw from the Breeze Inn. Nicknamed the Sleaze Inn, it was a grimy go-go bar with middle-aged dancers.

The Sleaze Inn wouldn't be open until four o'clock, and Ben Sherman would probably sleep until noon. Nick would have to wait a couple hours before he headed over there. His eyes fell on the middle of the paper, where he had scribbled "Roommates—Red Brick Tavern."

He snapped his phone open again. Holding down the number five on his phone, Nick speed-dialed Finn's number. "Any progress?" Nick asked when Finn picked up.

"Nothing good. So far, zero people saw Billy in the locker room. Most people were either hosing off their bikes or they were watching the awards ceremony."

Nick had a terrible feeling about this whole thing.

"The good news is that Tweety and I are only partway through the list."

"All right. I'm going to go see Jordan's roommates. Call me if anything comes up." Nick snapped close his phone and stuffed it in his pocket. He grabbed his gear and stalked out to the garage.

With a full tank of gas and boots that were still damp from the night before, Nick took off into the woods. The trail that led to the north side of town connected with the logging roads and ran past the abandoned quarry. After an open stretch, speeding along the dirt road, Nick turned into the quarry and nosed his bike down a huge gravel drop, letting the back end hang out as he got to the bottom. He came to a stop, perpendicular to the gravel pile, and then followed the edge of the quarry to the backside of the municipal dump.

The dump always smelled ripe, especially in the summer. Today was no exception. Nick sped by, racing away from the stench. Finally breathing fresh air, he crossed over the highway, which is illegal, but the only way to get over to the north side of town on a dirt bike. Nick wasn't old enough for a driver's license, and his Honda CRF150R wasn't registered or insured for riding on the street.

Hopefully, there aren't any cops around. Nick scanned the area. He rode through a small field at a diagonal and came out into the parking lot behind the Scrub and Bubble. The brand-new laundromat was very popular and for a good reason. There were two huge flat-screen TVs, one at each end of the large open room filled with washers and dryers.

The Scrub and Bubble played a newly released DVD every week, so people wouldn't be bored while they waited for their clothes. The parking lot was filled with cars. Some people weren't even doing their laundry, but came here just to watch the free movie.

The most exciting thing in this town is the laundromat, Nick thought. *That's so sad.* Nick had heard Kat's mom complain that one stinky old guy was there every day, even though the same movie played all day for seven days straight. It didn't seem to matter to him. That smelly old man would watch the same movie forty times.

"And he really needs to wash his clothes, but he never does," Kat's mom had said.

Nick used his U-lock to secure the bike to a lamppost. He walked across Scrub and Bubble's parking lot to the alley next to the Red Brick Tavern. He opened the gate that led to the Dumpsters, and came out at the back of the building.

There were a few very straggly bushes and a wooden staircase that went up to the second-floor apartment above the restaurant. Nick climbed the stairs, taking them two at a time, and knocked on the peeling paint of the light blue door.

"You're early!"

The door flew open. A girl, maybe in her twenties, stood wearing only a white terrycloth bath towel. The ends of her wet blond hair grazed her shoulders. Nick stared as one bead of water rolled down her arm, leaving a wet trail on her skin.

"Oh." She obviously had been expecting someone else. "Can I help you?"

Nick searched for words. He tried to remember why he was there. He tried, but all he could think of was how he wanted to be that bead of water.

"Are you lost?" The girl stared at him.

Why do people always think that? Nick thought. *Do I look lost?* Actually, he didn't want to know what he looked liked. Standing in front of him was one of the most beautiful girls he had ever seen up close, and she was practically naked. He was probably drooling.

Pull it together, man!

"Are you selling Boy Scout cookies?" The girl was holding the towel closed with one hand in front of her chest. The tension in the fabric went a little slack and Nick tried not to stare at the extra centimeter or so of skin that was exposed as she shifted her weight, still holding the door open with her other arm.

Nick felt hot and he knew he was blushing. Even the tips of his ears burned.

"Uh, that's the Girl Scouts. I think the boys collect canned food."

"I don't have any canned food. Sorry."

She smiled at him and the towel slipped another centimeter.

Nick felt woozy. "Are you Jordan Graham's roommate?" Nick stammered, his tongue tripping a couple times over the *J*.

The girl tensed. "Who wants to know?"

"I'm a friend of Billy Mackenzie. I was hoping you could . . ."

"Could what?" She adjusted the towel and glared at him. "Your friend is a murderer! What were you hoping I could do for you?"

Nick mentally kicked himself for not having a better plan. Of course she wouldn't want to help Billy. The police had told her Billy was the killer! *So stupid!*

"Who is it, Kayla? A tall dark-haired girl stepped into the doorway beside her.

"This Boy Scout says he's a friend of Billy Mackenzie," Kayla said through gritted teeth as her eyes flooded with tears.

"Just get out of here, kid. Leave us alone. We already told the police everything." The dark-haired girl put a protective arm around Kayla's bare shoulders. "Jordan told me she was going to the races to break up with Captain America. And now she's dead!" Her lip curled as she glared at him.

Nick didn't know what to say. He stared at the two girls mourning their friend and tried to make sense of what they were saying.

"Kayla? Gabby? Is everything okay?" Ben Sherman stood at the bottom of the stairs looking up at Nick.

"Is this guy bothering you?" Ben climbed the stairs two at a time, and when he reached the top landing, he towered over Nick.

He was a head taller and outweighed Nick by at least 120 pounds. He was wearing black cargo pants and a loose gray T-shirt. His huge arm muscles bulged out from the short sleeves.

"Yes," Gabby said. "He's bothering Kayla with questions about Jordan."

Ben wrapped his fingers underneath Nick's chest protector and lifted him six inches off the landing.

"From now on, for your own safety, I recommend you leave these ladies alone. And quit asking questions." He turned, carrying Nick away from the apartment door.

Ben dropped him, and Nick grabbed on to the railing to stop himself from stumbling down the stairs. Ben pulled his shirt up, exposing a gun stuffed into his waistband.

"Don't come around here again, kid, or you will get hurt. Now scram."

Nick didn't even look back. He ran to his bike. He had some difficulty getting his U-lock undone, mainly because his hands were shaking out of control. His brain was flooded with adrenaline—not the good kind that came with racing, but the bad kind that accompanied terror.

After being threatened by a gun-toting drug addict, Nick didn't really want to be home alone. He couldn't talk to Kat in the state he was in. He was trying to be strong for her, and if he saw her now, he might fall apart and bawl like a baby. That wouldn't be helpful.

He cut through the quarry and veered right off the trail and headed for Finn's house.

"Ah, the young Mr. Bishop!" Morris Foley, Finn's grandfather, opened the door and invited Nick in with a grand gesture, sweeping his arm down across his body and ending in a little bow. Mr. Foley was a very thin man with a shock of bright white hair, full beard, and mustache. Nick always thought he looked like a very skinny Santa. "Finnegan! Nick is here!"

"Coming!" Finn's voice came from somewhere upstairs.

"Are you hungry, Nick?" Morris went back to the kitchen counter, where he was slicing bananas and strawberries.

"Yeah, I am, actually." Nick peeled off his gear and then pulled himself up onto a kitchen stool.

He was feeling almost normal. The ride had taken his mind off Ben's gun, and relief washed over him in the Foley kitchen.

"What is that?" Nick watched Finn's grandfather pour a beige-colored substance over the fruit in the blender.

"Silken tofu!"

Nick curled his lip and shook his head. He had to shout when Mr. Foley turned the blender on. "Is it safe to eat?"

The whirring of the blender stopped. "Perfectly safe." Morris poured the light pink liquid into a glass and held it out to Nick. "It's a smoothie."

Nick took the pink drink and eyed it suspiciously.

"Tastes like chicken," Morris said, smiling. The old man drank from his own glass, leaving the bottom half of his white mustache glistening pink.

Finn bounded down the stairs. He looked

hopefully at the blender, and his grandfather filled two more glasses. Nick watched Finn gulp down the drink.

Looks safe enough, Nick thought. So he tentatively dipped his tongue into the liquid. It tasted like strawberries. *Chicken? Grown-ups are so weird sometimes.* They took the drinks upstairs to the computer, where Tweety was hanging up the phone. Finn handed him a smoothie of his own.

"Milkshake?"

"Yeah. Sort of," Finn lied. "So, what did they say?"

"Nothing. We've called ninety people so far, and no one saw Billy in or by the locker room. Kat has the rest of the list, but she hasn't had any luck either. Everybody was watching the podium." Tweety sat back and gulped down his pink drink.

"That's disgusting!" he said when he finished, sticking his tongue far out of his mouth.

"Why did you drink all of it then?" Finn rolled his eyes.

"You know me. I'll eat anything." Tweety wiped his mouth with his sleeve.

"You guys, can we get serious?" Nick paced back and forth across the room, and he told them everything he had learned so far. He told them about the newspaper article, Kevin, Gabby, Kayla, and Ben.

"So then he shows me this gun he's got, and tells me if I don't stay away from Kayla I'm going to get hurt."

"Get out of here!" Finn's eyes were wide. "What did you do?"

"What did I do? I ran. Are you kidding me? What

was I supposed to do?"

"And this girl, Kayla, answered the door in nothing but a towel?" Tweety asked. They lost him to a moment of daydreaming.

"Tweety! That is not important. The important parts of the story are that Jordan told her other roommate that she was going to break up with Billy. That girl Gabby told the police. And now the police are sure Billy killed Jordan in a jealous rage."

Nick sighed in exasperation. "Meanwhile, the person who probably did kill Jordan, just threatened me with a gun and almost threw me down a flight of stairs." Nick raised his voice more than he meant to, and he almost shouted the last sentence. His hands were shaking again. He leaned against the wall and slid down to the floor.

"Why would Ben kill Jordan?" Finn asked.

"Kevin said Ben was the one who was jealous. Billy stole his thunder, and Jordan liked Billy better." Nick shrugged. "If there is anybody who would kill in a jealous rage, it's this Ben Sherman guy.

"And now he's shacked up with the hot roommate while Billy's in jail? That sucks," Tweety said.

"Yeah, I got the feeling he and Kayla were together."

"Yeah, the whole half-naked thing at the door suggests a relationship." Tweety looked like he might have visions of terrycloth dancing in his head.

"Do you think he would hurt Kayla?" Finn asked.

"It's possible. We need to find out as much as we can about this guy, but we can't just go around knocking on doors. We need to be smarter about this. If he knows we're still asking questions, things could get very ugly very fast."

"Guys, we could be dealing with a serial killer here." Finn lost the color from his face and slumped to the floor.

"A serial killer?" Tweety threw his hands up in the air. "Why would you even think that?"

"Think about it. This guy, new in town, is interested in Jordan. She ends up dead. Now he's hanging around Kayla with a gun stuffed down his pants?"

"Finn could be right." Nick's stomach did a back flip as he imagined Kayla lying in a pool of her own blood. "We need to find out more about this guy. We need to find out where he came from."

Finn looked nervous. "Maybe we should go to the police with all of this. Don't you think it's a little, you know, over our heads?"

"Who are we going to talk to? Officer Tucker? Oh, yeah, he'd listen to us!" Nick shook his head. "No, the cops have made up their minds. You heard Kratchner, they think that Billy is the killer, and nothing a bunch of teenagers say to them is going to change their minds. We need to find proof—something substantial." Nick walked across the room. "Kratchner is not going to do anything. Tucker isn't going to do anything, and even our parents are acting like there is nothing they can do. But we can do something. We have to, or Kalya could end up dead, and Billy could end up in jail for the rest of his life."

Tweety was staring at his hands, but he nodded. Finn nodded too. "But what are we going to do?"

"First we are going to search Google, then we'll call Lakeview and find out which room is Ben's."

"Seriously, what did people do before the Internet?" Tweety marveled at the monitor.

They had started their Google search with questions like "how to spy on someone" and "how to do a criminal background check."

"Look at that. A night-vision hidden-camera teddy bear!" Finn leaned over Nick's shoulder pointing at the ugly stuffed animal.

"Or that hidden-camera alarm clock," Tweety said.

"There's a portable document scanner or a floating waterproof camera or, look, a digital recorder/pen." Tweety pointed farther down the screen.

"Too bad it's $300."

"We don't need that!" Finn said.

"What are we looking for then?" Tweety asked.

"We are looking for ideas. We need to know how to be good detectives." Nick sighed and scrolled down the page.

Nick could teach himself how to do things. He had learned how to tune his bike from watching his dad. He had learned how to adjust his suspension for races from instructional videos online. It was the same with learning freestyle motocross tricks. There were plenty of videos posted, some more helpful than others, but Nick managed to find valuable tips in a sea of dead ends and phony links.

"There's cell phone spy software, but it is definitely not in our budget," Nick said.

"What's our budget?" Finn asked.

"I have twenty dollars."

"Step back, Moneybags," Tweety said.

Finn straightened. "We'd need a credit card even for the background searches," he said.

"So I guess we can't afford the Covert Asset Tracker with GPS?" Tweety pointed at the screen.

"I would love to be able to track Ben Sherman with GPS, but no. We'll have to improvise," Nick said. He continued to search online. He typed in "how to take fingerprints." Finn went downstairs to try to find snacks. He came back with unsweetened granola and unsalted peanuts.

"How can you stand this?" Tweety asked through a mouthful of granola. "This tastes like crunchy cardboard!"

"You get used to it. I don't really even notice anymore." Finn took a handful from each bowl and mixed them in the palm of his hand.

"This is almost inedible," Tweety said through a mouthful of half-chewed granola.

"That won't stop you from eating it," Finn said.

"I said 'almost.'" Tweety shoveled another handful of granola into his mouth.

"Okay." Nick pointed at the screen. "This is what we need, and I bet we could get it all for under twenty dollars."

WEDNESDAY

"This is embarrassing," Finn said, scanning the aisles for anyone who might recognize them. "I am not going to be the one to pay for this! This is so stupid!"

Finn tossed the item in his hand to Nick. He had no reason to worry, the dusty Dollar Store was empty.

"Just relax. This is no big deal. Watch and learn." Tweety took the items from Nick and brought them up to the counter.

The woman at the register had straight strawlike hair and bright blue eyeliner clumped around her eyes. She smelled like an ashtray. Her green Dollar Store apron stretched tightly across her bony frame. A name tag announcing that her name was Charlene hung wonky and crooked off the pocket. She was flipping through the pages of *People*. She narrowed her eyes at Tweety and put the magazine down with a sigh to ring up his items.

"For my mom," Tweety said sweetly.

"Like I care." The lady rolled her eyes and then rang up the make-up brushes, black eye shadow, Scotch tape, a kitchen sponge, index cards, and clear plastic sandwich bags.

"See," Tweety said as they walked toward the exit. "No big deal."

When Nick went to push open the door, he froze.

"Wait!" He backtracked and hid behind a display of Fourth of July sparklers on sale at 60 percent off.

Nick signaled to Finn and Tweety to get out of sight with a wave of his hand and a hiss through his teeth.

"What is it?" Tweety craned his neck to look out

at the parking lot.

"That's Ben," Nick whispered.

"Ahh," Finn and Tweety said in unison.

Nick shifted his position to get a better look. He hoped the glare off the outside of the window would help hide him from being seen.

Ben was standing in the parking lot with a petite Latino girl, maybe in her twenties. He was leaning against a dark green Buick LeSabre. His shoulders were relaxed, and he had his hands in his pockets. The girl was only five feet tall, but she was obviously mad. She leaned into him with a pointed finger and poked his chest to emphasize whatever she was saying to him.

At first Ben stayed relaxed and kept his hands in his pockets. He was talking, and she stood with her hip jutted out to the side and her arms crossed over her chest. Her eyebrows were furrowed and her lips were pursed. She was fidgeting more and more as Ben talked, until her tightly held stance exploded into flailing arms making choppy gestures as she yelled at him. Nick could finally hear some of what she was screaming.

"You are lying! Why should I trust you?"

Ben lost his cool. He lurched toward her and grabbed both her arms. His tall, muscular frame towered over the slight girl. Nick could not hear what Ben was saying, but the girl's wide eyes and open mouth made him think she was scared or at least startled.

Ben lessened his grip on the girl's arms. She visibly relaxed. She nodded. Ben rubbed the girl's arms affectionately, and then they hugged. Ben kissed the girl's forehead. They headed into Slim's Irish Pub, Ben with his arm draped around her shoulders.

"What are you three doing?" Charlene stood with her hands on her hips, her bony elbows forming sharp angles out to the sides.

Tweety and Finn were crouched down behind the stack of beach towels in one window, and Nick was kneeling behind the rotating display of sunglasses.

"Well?" Charlene reached into the front pocket of her apron and pulled out a pack of Marlboro Reds.

Nick exchanged looks with Tweety and Finn. Nick could only imagine what they looked like, huddled by the windows, and he couldn't even begin to think up an excuse.

"Come on, get!" Charlene opened the door.

They all leapt up to their feet. Charlene stood in the doorway and lit her cigarette as she ushered them out.

"Freakin' kids."

"Was that Kayla or Gabby?" Tweety whispered as they walked around the other side of the strip mall.

"Neither. I don't know who that is," Nick said, pulling on his gear.

"I can see what you mean about Ben." Finn shivered. "He gives me the creeps."

"Yeah, it seems like he has a short fuse," Nick said.

"And multiple girlfriends!" Tweety stood next to his bike and pulled on his chest protector.

"That's why we need to find out more about him," Nick said.

"You didn't find anything on the Internet?" Finn asked.

"I found a ton of Ben Shermans, but there were no Ben Shermans listed in Colorado or San Diego."

"Oh, no posts for 'Ben Sherman: Serial Killer'?" Tweety said.

If only it were that easy.

Nick had a chill down his spine as he thought about what he had to do next. He shook it off and kick-started his bike.

THURSDAY

It was late in the afternoon the following day. They still had plenty of time, but they had to get into position before dark. They rode north parallel to the highway and pulled into the gas station parking lot. The last thing Nick wanted happening tonight was for any of them to run out of gas just when they needed it the most. They topped off all three tanks.

Nick checked for cars, cop cars in particular, and then they crossed over the highway. They rode with the setting sun to their backs through a few acres of field. Luckily, it was still early in the summer, and the fields had been brush-hogged last fall. By August, the scrub and hay would be five or six feet tall and impossible to ride through. The field turned to forest and the boys picked their way north through the trees.

Nick slowed down and did a tight U-turn. He swung his leg off the bike and leaned it up against a tree. Tweety and Finn pulled up next to Nick and did the same. They left their helmets propped up on their seats.

"We have to walk the rest of the way. I don't want to chance anybody hearing us. And if anything happens, get out of here as fast as possible. If we get separated, we'll meet back up at Finn's."

"I'm going to throw up."

Tweety did look a little green.

Nick smiled. For someone who was as fearless as Tweety on a dirt bike, he could be such a pansy off the track. On his Yamaha YZ85, Tweety would try any trick, no matter how dangerous, but crouching in the shadows of the woods, he looked terrified.

"Everything is going to be fine. Do you have your phones set on vibrate?"

Everyone checked their phones and nodded.

"Okay, let's go."

They walked through the woods until they could see the silhouette of Lakewood View Motel, black against the orange and pink sky. Nick nodded to Tweety and Finn. He snuck through the field to the side of the motel, while the other two headed to the Breeze Inn, careful to stay hidden in the woods until they heard from Nick.

Nick stayed low in the drainage ditch, twenty feet from the building. On the phone earlier, the manager had said Ben was in room number 7. Lakewood View only had seven rooms, and all the rooms' entrances faced Route 28, so it meant Ben was in the last room on the left. The window was slightly green, fluorescent bulbs glowing in the approaching twilight. A shadow figure passed by the window.

Ben is still in there.

Nick kicked himself for not calling Slim's and finding out which nights Ben worked. If Ben didn't leave his room, this all was a waste.

I suck at this detective stuff!

But Nick was more nervous than frustrated. He pulled out his phone and sent a text to Tweety.

HOLD.

Nick crawled on his belly in the ditch until he could see the door to number 7. He lay as flat as he could, also trying to hide himself from the constant traffic buzzing by on the highway. The scratchy crabgrass poked through his shirt and made his arms itch.

As he waited, Kayla flashed into his mind. If Ben was the killer, Kayla was in danger. He needed to warn her, but how? Then he found himself thinking about the two centimeters of curved flesh exposed by the towel, her arms and shoulders still wet from the shower. He thought of going back to her apartment to warn her.

Maybe she would drop that towel.

Nick shook that thought from his head.

Not helpful.

Then he thought of Kat. They had spoken that afternoon. Kat was able to get the Grahams' phone number from information but hadn't gotten through to them yet. Nick had told her about Ben and his argument with the girl in the parking lot but decided it was best to keep her in the dark about what he and the guys were up to tonight.

Kat had enough to worry about.

"My mom cries all the time, and she focuses on the worst-case scenario. I keep trying to reassure her, but she is so scared that Billy will be found guilty. Nothing else matters to her. That fear has taken hold of her and won't let go. I don't know what else I can do." Kat sucked in a ragged breath.

Nick had known she was crying on the other end.

"You are doing everything you can," Nick had said.

We all are.

Nick shifted his legs into a more comfortable position and watched the motel door. The sky was a dark deep blue and the full moon was rising over the trees. It looked huge. They had seen a moon like this when Finn's grandfather took them camping two years ago. He had explained that when you can compare the moon to other objects along the horizon, the moon looks bigger, and once it rises into the night sky it appears small. But it's just an optical illusion, he said. The moon is always the same size; only our perception changes.

Maybe Ben is going to stay in the whole night?

Nick was getting impatient. He was also starting to lose his nerve. His stomach did a flip, and Nick wiped his sweaty palms on his pant leg.

What was I thinking? Why did I think I could do this? Am I crazy?

He was just about to crawl back to the woods, when the door to number 7 swung open. Ben stood in the doorway, switched out the light, and locked the door behind him. His dark muscular figure ambled across the parking lot, headed straight for the Breeze Inn.

Nick sent Tweety another text.

GO.

A horrible hot acid flooded his mouth and burned the back of his throat. Every muscle in his body tensed as he waited another five minutes. Nick's heart was pounding away in his chest, and he jumped when his phone vibrated in his hand.

GO.

The text meant Tweety and Finn had seen Ben enter the go-go bar. They would stay on the lookout for when he was leaving, give Nick the signal, and Nick would have five minutes to get out. But first he had to break in, which he wasn't sure he could do.

This is it. Nick thought about Billy and Kat and Mrs. Mackenzie, and he knew he had to at least try.

Nick snuck up to number 7 and leaned against the door in the shadows. He pulled a long piece of plastic from his backpack. Earlier, he had cut three different pieces of varying length from a two-liter soda bottle. Each end was shaped slightly differently. There was a lot of information online, like different techniques for opening a locked door, and Nick came prepared to try all of them.

If Lakewood View was a newer building, or if anything in the ramshackle motel had been updated since the Nixon administration, Nick knew he'd never get the door open. Lucky for him, everything, including the locks, looked ancient.

He leaned against the powder blue door and slid the plastic strip in between the doorframe and the door. The plastic strip was even with the door handle. Nick pushed it in until it would not go any farther. He twisted the strip until it was touching the doorknob and pushed the strip farther in. He then pushed the remaining bit of plastic in the opposite direction and turned the knob. The door popped open.

"Holy shit!" Nick covered his mouth after the words slipped out.

It actually worked!

He hustled inside and locked the door behind him. The room was pitch-black. His heart was pounding. The throbbing filled his eardrums. After an internal debate, weighing the danger of being discovered versus not finding anything because he couldn't see in the pitch-black, Nick switched the lights on.

The room was like a time capsule. There was an avocado bedspread, wood paneling on the walls, and a puke-colored orange frame around the mirror. The room was neater than Nick had expected it to be. He had anticipated empty bottles and full ashtrays, but everything was fairly neat—not exactly clean, but clutter free. There was a faint musty old-building smell, somewhere in between milk gone bad and roadkill.

Not even exactly sure what he was looking for, Nick began to search. The desk drawer contained a phone book and a Bible, both motel standard issue. The dresser drawers were filled with folded shirts and pants, clean socks, and underwear. A light jacket was the only thing hanging in the closet. He checked under the bed and ran his hands under the pillows and the mattress.

The bathroom was empty except for a razor and a toothbrush. Nick eyed the dark, heavy shower curtain. He froze. His heart raced with a sudden sense that there was something—or someone—behind it. He held his breath and strained to listen. He felt strangled by his own fear. He forced himself to take a small step forward. He reached out and yanked open the curtain.

He stared at the empty tub. A ring of rust circled the drain. Nick leaned up against the wall and felt his knees goes weak. What had he expected to find?

A dead body in the tub?

Nick tried to laugh at himself as he caught his breath and willed his heart to stop exploding against his throat, but he failed to shake off the squeezing weight of his own fear.

He just had to keep moving despite the fear. He tugged the mirror to see if it was a medicine cabinet. It wasn't. Nick scanned the empty bathroom. There was a wall-mounted sink, a threadbare towel hanging from the towel rack, and a Pepto Bismol–pink toilet left with the seat up.

His eyes came to rest on the toilet. He folded down the seat and the lid and lifted off the ceramic cover from the back of the toilet. He starred down into the reservoir.

Nothing.

Well, there was a ring of rust at the water line and all the usual toilet parts, but nothing useful to Nick. Nothing that told Nick anything about this guy.

Nothing incriminating.

Nick put the heavy cover back on the tank and starred down, feeling beyond stupid.

Hopeless.

He was running out of time and he had taken all this risk, but he was no closer to knowing anything about Ben. And then Nick noticed something. At first it looked just like a smudge on the pink plastic toilet seat cover. But when Nick looked closer, he could see it was two distinct interlocking shapes.

Like sneaker treads!

Nick looked up at the low ceiling. He stepped up onto the toilet and gently lifted the panel above the toilet, peeking into the space created by the drop ceiling.

I knew it!

There was a stack of folders and papers hidden there. Nick's pulse was pounding away, making him a little lightheaded. He carefully pulled out the stack, stepped down, and sank to the floor to rifle through his find.

There were maps with routes marked, and papers

with diagrams and notes scribbled on them. Nick pulled out his phone and started taking pictures of everything in the stack. He was about halfway through the pile when his blood ran cold. There were pictures of Jordan. They looked like they had been taken from far away without her knowing. Ben had been stalking Jordan.

We were right! He's a serial killer.

He tried to keep his hands from shaking, and he took pictures as fast as he could. After six pictures of Jordan, Nick sucked his breath in again.

Kayla.

Picture after picture of Kayla.

She is in danger too!

There were pictures of a dozen other women in the pile. One of them Nick recognized as the girl arguing with Ben the day before, and another was Jordan's dark-haired roommate, Gabby. Nick finished up with the pile. The last few pictures were of trucks being loaded or unloaded.

What is going on here? Who is this crazy guy?

With trembling hands, Nick put the stack of papers back up into their hiding place behind the ceiling panel and examined the toilet seat cover to make sure he hadn't left a footprint of his own. He put the lid and the seat up, closed the shower curtain, and double-checked to make sure everything was exactly the way he had found it.

Nick went back into the bedroom and checked his phone. He wanted to get out of the room as fast as he could, but he had one more thing to do. From his backpack, Nick pulled out the black eye shadow and a make-up brush. There were visible smudges on the glossy enamel veneer of the dresser. He loaded the brush up with eye shadow and swiped it back and forth over the dresser drawer. He put the powder away and retrieved the Scotch tape, index cards, and plastic bag.

Checking his phone every few seconds and struggling to keep his hands from shaking, Nick carefully spread tape over the distinct fingerprints on the drawer face. With each piece of tape, he lifted off a clear fingerprint. Nick laminated each print by sticking the tape to the back of an index card and dropping each one into the plastic bag. He pulled out the kitchen sponge, wet it in the bathroom sink, and wiped the dresser clean. Everything went back into his pack.

Nick turned off the lights, made sure the door was locked behind him, and ran back to the drainage ditch. He fell to his knees and puked in the grass. He spit, trying to get rid of the bad taste in his mouth. The moonlight shone down on the puddle of sick. Nick rolled away from it and lay flat on his back on the spiky crabgrass. He couldn't think straight because of the pounding of his heart and the flood of adrenaline making his head spin.

Nick stared up at the night sky. The navy-black was spotted with brilliant stars. A tiny flashing red dot crossed the sky. Nick wondered where that plane was headed.

New York, maybe? DC?

The night was perfectly still. The cold sweat was evaporating from Nick's forehead. He had finally slowed his racing heart, when a gunshot rang out in the dark woods behind the motel.

Tweety and Finn!

Nick bolted upright and, without thinking, ran toward the sound. He got to the tree line and dodged in and around trees. He headed in the direction of the go-go bar. He heard voices, shouting, and people running in the woods. Another gunshot rang out in the darkness very nearby.

Nick froze.

"Stop shooting!" a man shouted in the shadows. "It's just a couple of kids."

"What if they heard something?" The voice of the shooter was a woman.

"Relax. They were probably just trying to sneak a peek at the dancers." The man sounded familiar, but Nick couldn't see anything from where he was, and he didn't dare move.

"This is not a game. This is not a damn slumber party!" The woman's voice was now clenched and severe. But Nick strained to hear because the woman's voice sounded familiar too. "It is too late to turn back now. We won't get another chance at this!"

"I get it. But Maya had a point. How will it work without Jordan?"

"Listen, as far as I'm concerned, you're an outsider. I'm not happy you're here. So stop sniffing around into what doesn't concern you!"

"All right, just take it easy. You're really wound tight, you know that?" The man sighed. "Put the gun away. They're gone."

The two people sounded like they were twenty or thirty feet away. Nick was crouched down behind a tree, trying not to make a sound. He could hear his heart beating loudly in his eardrums, and he tried to push the panicky fear pounding in his head down to a dull hum so he could hear them talk. Their voices grew distant, and Nick could only hear a few murmurs. Then it was quiet.

Leaves rustled as a breeze blew through the trees, and Nick was grateful he had already thrown up. He took a deep breath and reached his hand out, balancing against a tree as he stood up. His legs were weak beneath him. He heard a noise, a twig snapping behind him, and he whirled around.

The moon was bright, but it only illuminated patches of the forest floor; the rest was carpeted in deep shadows cast by the canopy of leaves above. Nick saw only dark shapes, unmoving in the trees.

Get a grip, Nick told himself. *I have to get out of here before I scare myself to death.*

Nick squinted one more time into the darkness, and turned around to get back to his bike. From the darkness behind him, a hand clamped down on Nick's mouth, and an arm wrapped around him in an iron grip.

"Do not move. Do not make a sound."

"Do you have a death wish, kid?" Nick realized where he had heard the man's voice before. It was Ben Sherman. Nick's mind was racing in all different directions. His brain felt like it might burst apart with questions. *How did Ben know I was here? Does he know I was in his room? Is he going to kill me now?*

In the middle of total panic and terror, Nick had one clear thought that wiped all the others away. It was weird. He thought of Kat. If he died here and now, he'd never prove Billy was innocent, and he'd disappoint her. It was a hollow feeling. *Total and utter failure.*

Ben shook him. "I do not know what you are up to, but you are messing with the wrong people." Ben spun Nick around and shoved him flat up against the tree, still holding his hand tightly over Nick's mouth. "This is not kid's stuff. Now get out of here! And I do not want to see your face again. Are we clear?"

Nick nodded his head.

"Now run." Ben shoved Nick from the tree.

Nick ran. The dark woods around him seemed to pass in a blur. His brain was flooded with numbing, blinding fear. He didn't dare look over his shoulder, afraid that at any moment Ben would shoot him in the back. He passed behind the motel, but he was farther east, deeper in the woods than he had been before. He had to cut right to get back to the bikes. Smashing through the branches, Nick ran at full speed.

Nick's boot caught on something. The side of his face smacked a tree as he fell forward. His lip smashed on a rock as he hit the ground. Splayed out on the forest floor, he saw stars floating in front of his eyes, and pain shot through his cheekbone.

It took a long minute for Nick to lift his head up. He pushed up off his stomach and tried to pull his legs up underneath him so he could get to his feet, but he was dizzy and his one foot was tangled up in something. He couldn't get it loose.

Resting his head down for a minute, Nick caught his breath. He ran his tongue over his teeth, making sure they were still all there. He rolled over to get a look at what his foot was caught on. He sat up and a double vision of shadow and light crisscrossed in front of him. He closed his eyes and held his head. Reaching down to feel what entangled his foot, Nick's hands found fabric—cotton jersey.

Nick struggled to unwrap the fabric from around the side buckle of his riding boot. The fabric was partially wet and attached to something cold and heavy. Nick had a sick and horrible drop in his stomach. He opened his eyes. When his vision cleared, he could see that his boot, illuminated in a small pool of bright moonlight, was caught on a bloody T-shirt. The girl wearing the T-shirt was lying facedown, dead.

"Nick! Where were you? What—?" Finn burst through the trees and stopped midsentence.

Tweety came running from behind Finn, and the two of them stood frozen, staring at Nick and the girl lying on the forest floor.

"I can't believe this. Is she dead?" Tweety asked, still not moving.

Finn stepped forward and knelt down. He untangled Nick's boot.

"Finn, I don't know if you should touch her."

Tweety grabbed Nick by his shirt and one arm, and he hoisted Nick to his feet.

"We have to see if she's still alive," Finn said.

"She feels"—Nick choked back a gag—"cold."

Finn put two fingers on the underside of her wrist, and sat silently.

"Yeah, she's dead." Finn cocked his head and leaned down toward the dead girl's face. His jaw dropped.

"You guys are not going to believe this." Finn jumped away from the body. "I think it's that girl, the girl fighting with Ben in the parking lot."

"Shh!" Nick said. He was filled with panic and searched the dark shadows around them.

"Let's get out of here!" Tweety grabbed Nick by the sleeve. "Let's go!"

"Tweety, we can't. We have to call the police," Finn said.

"Finn's right. I'll stay," Nick said. "You guys go."

"No way. Next thing we know Tucker will arrest you for murder too," Finn said. "We all have to stay."

"Tucker is going to arrest him any way when he sees that Nick has a set of makeshift burglary tools in his backpack!" Tweety threw up his arms.

"Okay, here's what we do." Nick spoke in a whisper. "Tweety, you take my backpack, and my phone. I found stuff in Ben's room and took pictures, so be careful with it." Nick's mind was foggy, but the gears were moving again.

"Finn and I will stay here and call the police. We'll get our bikes and ride them over here, and we can say that's how we found her." Nick scanned the dark shadows. Fear pressed in on him from all sides.

As they walked through the woods back to their bikes, he fought to keep his head clear. He wanted to just lie down, but he kept moving one foot in front of the other, following Finn through the darkness.

Tweety took Nick's pack and jumped on his bike, the motor filled the quiet night with its roar. Nick's hands were shaking as he fastened his helmet strap under his chin. His legs felt weak, like he had run a hundred miles. He threw all his weight on to the kick-start lever and rolled the throttle, but the engine didn't turn over.

Come on! Nick thought. *Start!* Nothing. Nick was dirt tired. He just wanted to give up and go to sleep right there on the ground. He had to shake off this fog in his brain. Tweety and Finn were waiting for him. He tried the kick-start again, and this time the motor turned over. He gave the guys the thumbs-up sign.

Tweety waved and rode away toward home, and Nick and Finn rode back to the girl's cold, lifeless body. Seeing her bloody and alone in the bluish-white moonlight sent a chill down Nick's spine. Ben's threatening voice echoed in his mind.

Finn dialed 911. Nick got off his bike and sat down with his back against a tree. One minute his limbs each weighed a hundred pounds, but as he listened to Finn talk, it felt like he was floating, watching the scene from above.

What is going on here? Nick tried to organize his suspicions. *It has to be Ben.* But then why would he send Nick running in the direction of the body? What was Ben up to? Why did Ben have photos of Jordan and her roommates? And who was the girl with gun? What were they doing that it was too late to turn back now? What wouldn't they get another chance at?

Who were they? Nick's head pounded. He couldn't think anymore. The police arrived and Finn helped Nick up to his feet. Bright flashlights blinded Nick, and he shielded his eyes.

"I do not believe this!" Officer Tucker's voice came from behind one of the piercing lights. "Am I to believe that this is just a coincidence? Am I to believe that you kids are just corpse magnets? This is the second dead body you have found in a week!"

Tucker stalked up to the two boys, keeping his oversize Maglite trained on their faces. "What have you got yourselves involved in?"

The boys squinted into the glaring whiteness.

"What are you doing out here in the woods at night?"

"We go for night rides. We've got headlights," Finn said. Nick could feel Tucker's eyes burrowing through him, as if the flashlight beam illuminated their lies as clearly as it illuminated their faces.

"What happened to you?" Tucker asked.

"Oh." Nick reached up and felt abrasions on his cheek, "I tripped. Over her."

"If you were riding, how did you trip over the body?"

Nick's mouth hung open. He didn't know what to say.

"Nature calls?" Finn offered with a shrug.

A wave of icy silence hit them full force, and both boys stood perfectly still as it washed over them.

"You are not funny," Tucker finally said, and he swung his light off them and headed to the body. "Do not move from that spot."

"Thanks for letting us sleep over, Mr. Foley." Nick held an ice pack to the side of his face. His cheek and eye were swollen and the skin had already started to turn a deep purple color.

"You have had quite an ordeal. Besides, your father will see that tomorrow. You are only delaying the inevitable," Finn's grandfather said.

Sometimes Nick thought that Morris Foley could see right through him, that he almost knew what he was thinking. It was disturbing when it happened. Nick was used to being mostly invisible at home.

"This should help with the bruising." He handed Nick a tube of arnica gel.

"Thanks." Nick took the tube and went upstairs.

Finn was pacing back and forth across his bedroom floor, and Tweety was sitting on the floor with his head in his hands.

"What happened back there?" Tweety whispered as he shut the door behind Nick.

"Tucker grilled us on why we were out there." Nick was beyond exhausted. It had been five days since they found Jordan's body, but it felt like two lifetimes.

"He didn't believe a word we said, but he couldn't think of a reason why we would kill her. So he let me call my grandfather to come get us," Finn said.

"Who was she?" Tweety asked.

Nick shrugged. "The police said her name was Anna Rael."

"We told Tucker about Ben's fight with her in the parking lot," Finn said.

"Yeah, but I don't think he believed that either."

Nick adjusted the ice pack. "What I couldn't tell him was that Ben has pictures of Jordan, Anna, Kayla, Gabby, and a bunch of other girls in his room."

"Sounds like a serial killer," Tweety said. "What else did you find?"

"No, no—first, what happened to you? Why were they shooting at you?" Nick asked, keeping his voice down.

Finn and Tweety looked at each other. Finn nodded, gesturing to Tweety to tell the story.

"We were watching the entrance of the go-go place, just like we planned. Ben walked over from the motel." Tweety stared at the floor as he spoke. "We sent you a text, and then we waited."

"Nothing happened for about a half hour," Finn added. "Then all of a sudden, a window breaks."

"Somebody broke it from the inside, and we could hear all this yelling. So Finn starts creeping closer." Tweety glared up at Finn.

"I wanted to hear what they were saying."

"And you almost got us killed!"

"I did not. You are . . ."

"Guys!" Nick stepped in between them. "Stop, okay? Did you hear anything?"

"Yeah, there was a guy and a girl," Tweety continued. "Ben and the nutcase who shot at us."

"And there was another woman, but we couldn't see her, we could only hear her voice."

"The woman was saying, 'But what about Jordan, how is it going to work without her?'"

"And then the nutcase lady got really mad."

"Yeah, she threw a glass or something. We heard it shatter. And she said, 'Forget about Jordan. Just stick to the plan.' And then"—Tweety scowled at Finn—"Finn knocked over a garbage can!"

"I didn't see it! It was dark, and I was trying to get closer so I could see the woman's face."

"Anyway, the one chick pulls out a gun and shoots at us through the window! We booked out of there as fast as we could."

"We ran back to the woods by the hotel and texted you, but you didn't come out. So we went back to the bikes to see if you were already there, but you weren't."

"We were freaking out that you had gotten caught, and we didn't know what to do."

Tweety put his head down in his hands.

"I was scared shitless. Seriously, man." He looked up and shook his head. "And then we found you."

"And the body," Finn added.

Nick nodded; the pieces of the night were coming together in his mind.

"That's what happened to us. What happened to you?" Finn asked.

Nick told them about finding the maps and pictures and hearing the gunshot. He told them about getting grabbed by Ben. He showed them the pictures on the phone and pulled all the laminated fingerprints out of his backpack.

"What is all of this about?" Finn asked as he flipped through the images on Nick's phone. "What are in these trucks? What was Jordan mixed up in?"

"And what do we do now?" Tweety moved to the edge of the bed.

I have no idea, thought Nick.

"We need help."

Besides Tweety, Egghead was the only Clark boy still at home. He attended West Central Community College and worked part-time at Dave's Carwash on the north side of town. Wile E. and Bosko shared an apartment across the county line and worked for an excavating company.

"They like to play in the dirt, always have," Mr. Clark would say of his two oldest sons.

Rocky had joined the Navy and was stationed on an aircraft carrier somewhere in the Gulf, and Mugsy was on the East Coast for the summer after his first year at Carnegie Mellon, working at the university's computer lab. The family joked that Mugsy was a flake, but Nick knew for a fact that he was pretty much a genius. Or at least seriously book smart and a computer genius. He got a perfect score on his SATs and he received a full academic scholarship to one of the best computer engineering programs in the country. But *all* of the Clark brothers could be counted on in a pinch.

"Tweety, I need to talk to Mugsy. Can you get him on the phone? Finn, can you scan these?" Nick handed Finn the fingerprints.

Finn went over to the computer and turned the scanner on. He arranged the laminated fingerprints tape-side down, and imported them into the computer. Nick emailed himself the photos from his phone, and printed the photos from the e-mail.

"So do you think you can find his criminal record with these prints?" Tweety was on the phone with his brother.

It was almost midnight Mountain Standard Time

and three in the morning on the East Coast, but Mugsy was a night owl.

"I will certainly try—anything to help Billy. It will be harder if this guy is using a fake name. It would be easier to do a search on this guy if you had grabbed his driver's license," Mugsy said on the other end of line.

"I'm so sorry, next time we break into someone's hotel room, we'll try to remember to steal the guy's wallet, too!" Tweety smacked his forehead with the heel of his hand, and Nick grabbed the phone away from him.

"Mugs, it's Nick. We need more information on this guy, and anything you find will be really helpful."

"No problem. I've got a buddy who can hack into databases in his sleep." There was a pause on the line. "Did you guys really break into this guy's hotel room?"

Nick sighed. He realized how bad it sounded when Mugsy said it out loud. He thought about lying, but he was just too tired. "Yeah."

"That is seriously badass, Bishop. I'm impressed."

Nick smiled, and it hurt his face.

"I'll get back to you as soon as I find something." And the line went dead.

Nick closed the phone, tossed it to Tweety, and collapsed on Finn's bed.

FRIDAY

Sunlight pierced through the window and poked Nick in the eye. He rolled over to get away from it and cried out in pain when the left side of his face touched the pillow. When he sat up, his whole head started pounding. His jaw, his lips, and his left cheek were killing him. He couldn't open his left eye all the way.

"Uuuhhhhhh," he moaned as he tried to move his jaw around. Swinging his legs off the edge of the bed, Nick felt a wave of dizziness and nausea. From the bedside table, Nick grabbed the arnica gel and smeared it on his face. The coolness of the clear gel eased his pain a little.

He heard voices in the kitchen. Fighting for balance, Nick shuffled downstairs to the kitchen and stood, shoulders slumped, in the doorway.

"Wow. Does that feel as bad as it looks?" Finn was sitting at the kitchen counter.

"It's worse." Nick leaned against the doorframe, blinking stars from his vision.

"I highly doubt that," Tweety said, shaking his head. He came up close and examined Nick's face. "It looks like somebody put your face through a meat grinder."

"I mean, I think I have a concussion." Nick held his head.

"Don't let my grandfather hear you say that! We will have to spend all day at the hospital, and then some dumb doctor will say, 'Yep. You've got a concussion all right. Too bad we can't do anything about it.' It will burn the entire day."

"I know, I know." As Nick got used to the pain in

his face, other aches and pains began to emerge. He lifted his shirt, and there was a deep purple bruise down his left side where he had collided with the hard earth after tripping over the dead girl's body.

"That was crazy double-O-seven stuff last night. We should show everything you found to Kat," Tweety said.

"We were just waiting for you to wake up before we headed over to her house," Finn said. "But, if you do have a concussion, you definitely shouldn't ride."

"Even if you don't have a concussion, I don't think you can fit a helmet over your fat swollen face. I'll call Egghead to come and get us."

"Do you think we could make one stop on the way?" Nick held his ribs and sat at the kitchen counter.

Tweety shrugged. "I don't see why not."

Finn's grandfather walked in from outside. He always got up at the crack of dawn and did yoga in the woods or meditated or something. "Good morning, boys. You want some breakfast?" Mr. Foley pulled a pot from a lower cabinet.

"Sure. Got any Cocoa Puffs?" Tweety asked, even though they all knew the answer was no. Nick had seen this little ritual before, whenever Tweety was over.

"Coming right up!" Finn's grandfather said, as he started preparing hot quinoa, a whole grain that tasted like cardboard, sprinkled with ground almonds and prunes. "Wah-lah! Keen-wah!" The old man placed the steaming bowls of cereal in front of the boys with a little bow and a dramatic wave of his hand. Nick forced a smile, but it hurt his face.

"Why do you want to stop at the Red Brick?" Egghead asked as he pulled away from Finn's house. Tweety and Finn were in the tiny fold-down seat in the back of Egghead's truck, kicking each other in a struggle for more legroom. Nick was in the front staring out the window.

"I have to warn Kayla. If Ben is the killer, she could be next."

He had printed out one of the photos from his phone. It was one of Ben's stalker photos of Kayla. He put it in an envelope with a note that said: *Someone is watching you. Be careful.*

When they pulled up behind the Red Brick Tavern, Kayla's car was parked next to the building. The rest of the parking lot was empty, except for a black SUV with tinted windows parked on the far side of the parking lot.

"It's okay, that's not Ben's car," Nick said. "He drives a crappy LaSabre."

"If Ben sees you here again, he will kill you for sure," Tweety said.

Nick thought that was true, but if Kayla was in danger, someone had to warn her. All these terrible things were happening around her, the same terrible things that were happening around him. The difference was that Kayla trusted the one person who could hurt her the most. Nick bristled with the thought of Ben manipulating Kayla, lying to her while he made plans to hurt her.

"I have to warn her," Nick said.

"I think someone's in love," Tweety said in a singsong voice.

"I think he's hoping she'll open the door naked this time," Finn said.

Tweety thought about that for a second.

"Maybe I should go? Give me that. I'll take it to her." Tweety reached for the envelope, but Nick pulled it out of his reach.

"Knock it off, this is serious. If she answers the door, I can't give her the photo, because if she knows it came from me and Ben saw it . . ."

"He would know you broke into his room, and he would find you and kill you," Egghead supplied.

Nick nodded. "Right."

"So, if she answers the door, what are you going to say?" Finn asked.

"I guess something will come to me." Nick put the envelope in his back pocket and got out of the truck.

"If Ben answers the door, I suggest you say a quick Hail Mary," Tweety said.

Nick climbed the back stairs and knocked on Kayla's door. The sun seemed impossibly bright. It hurt his left eye, and Nick felt sweat bead up on his scalp and on his palms. The door swung open, and Kayla did a double take at Nick's pummeled face.

"What happened to you, Boy Scout?" Kayla asked.

She was wearing a tight red strapless tube top, and her hair was swept up into a loose ponytail. Her white cotton pants were slung low on her hips, leaving an expanse of skin from her belly button to the tops of her hip bones exposed.

Nick ignored the question and started talking without thinking.

"Listen, I know Jordan was up to something, something illegal or dangerous. I don't know what, but I think it got her killed, and you could be in danger too!"

Kayla rolled her eyes and went to close the door, but Nick stopped it with his hand.

"Kayla, wait! I'm sorry. Look, I know you don't believe me, but Billy did not kill Jordan! And I know I don't know you, but I don't want anything bad to happen to you."

Kayla stepped closer to him and studied his face. Nick tried to find somewhere to set his gaze, but with her that close, it was a minefield.

Eyes? No, way too intense. Exposed neck and shoulder? Nope!

He did not want Kayla to think he was ogling her. The curves under the tube top were definitely out of the question.

Belly button. No, don't look at that! Hip bone? No, not there!

Nothing was safe, so Nick tried to look at the spot right in between her eyes, occasionally letting his gaze slipped down to her full, soft lips.

"I know you think Billy killed Jordan. And I know you don't have any reason to believe me, but I think Ben could hurt you." Nick let his eyes meet hers.

"That's impossible. Ben loves me." Kayla threw her shoulders back, standing taller. She went from all hard lines to sweet softness. She smiled. Nick felt an ache deep inside him that had nothing to do with his injuries. She was so soft and angelic and fierce and strong, all at the same time. Nick wished he had an excuse to reach out and touch her.

"My life is . . . complicated, but I'm a big girl." She lowered her head and looked at Nick from under her thick, dark lashes. "I know what I'm doing."

"You are sweet to worry about me, though." Her full lips pulled away from each other as she smiled at him again.

"Kayla, please listen to me. It's not just Jordan. I think Ben killed another woman too."

"Another woman?" She stiffened. Something changed in her face. "Who?"

"I don't think you know her—Anna Rael. But Ben definitely knew her."

"Why do you think that?" She narrowed her eyes at Nick.

"I saw them arguing. He is a dangerous guy. You just have to trust me. I think you're in danger."

"I mean, why do you think Anna is dead?" The color was draining out of Kayla's face.

"We found her body in the woods last night."

"You found her body?" Kayla faltered a bit in the doorway, like her knees were going out from under her. She gripped the doorjamb.

Nick started to reach out to her, but she snapped at him.

"Maybe you killed her?"

Nick starred speechless at her.

"You don't believe that," Nick finally said.

"Get out of here, kid," she said softly. "And if you know what's good for you, don't come back."

She shut the door in his face.

"How'd that go?" Finn asked when Nick climbed back into the truck.

"I'm not really sure." Nick stared straight ahead, trying to figure out what would make Kayla react so strangely. If she knew Anna too, what did that mean?

"Bishop's never seen a girl naked before." Tweety patted Nick on the shoulder. "It can lead to a confusing swell of feelings."

Egghead rolled his eyes. "Like you'd know."

"She had all her clothes on," Nick said.

"Better luck next time."

"She also knew Anna Rael." Nick turned to face his friends. " Two of the girls that Ben photographed are now dead. I think the girls all know one another somehow. And I think they are all involved with something very dangerous."

Kat came running out of the front door as Egghead
pulled his pickup into the Mackenzies' driveway.
Today, she was wearing a tight yellow T-shirt that
read STRANGERS HAVE THE BEST CANDY.

"What happened to your face?"

"Ah, it's nothing. You should see the other guy,"
Nick said, but he grunted in pain as he stepped down
from the truck, and he was limping slightly as he
walked toward the house—which definitely ruined his
tough-guy routine.

Tweety, Finn, and Egghead piled into the house.
Kat stopped Nick on the front steps and touched the
side of his swollen face. It hurt and he winced. Kat
pulled her hand away.

"Come on inside," she said. "We have to be quiet
because my mom is lying down. She's been such a
wreck. I think she's making herself sick."

They were all spread out around the Mackenzies'
living room. Egghead and Kat were on the couch.
Tweety and Finn were on the floor by the coffee
table, and Nick was in the brown recliner with bags of
ice on his ribs and face.

"Are you sure nothing is broken?"

"He's fine, Kat. Plus, his ugly face is the least of
our concerns."

"Thanks, Tweety." Nick stifled a laugh, because
laughing hurt too much.

"Tweety's right. We've got to all put our heads
together and figure out what's going on here. What
are these people up to? How is Ben Sherman
involved, and why did he kill these two girls?" Finn
spread the printouts of the pictures all over the coffee

table.

Finn and Tweety had already relayed the events of the past few days, and they were hoping that brainstorming as a group would help them put together the puzzle pieces.

"Ben marked these maps along the Interstate. He also marked a route north of the quarry, which isn't a road on the map but could be one of the dirt logging roads."

"There are two or three up there that intersect with the highway." Egghead leaned forward and took the printout, inspecting it closer. Kat picked up a printout of the trucks being loaded.

"I can't quite make out what it says on these boxes."

"Some of the pictures are a little blurry, because my hands were shaking," Nick said from underneath the ice pack.

"I can not believe you guys broke into this guy's motel room." Egghead shook his head. "And you didn't even invite me! Next time you do a B&E, I'm there!"

Kat scowled. "Don't even joke around," she said. "You guys do not need to break any more laws. What would I do if all of you were sitting in jail along with Billy?"

She got up from the couch and came back with a magnifying glass.

"B-Tec Pharmaceuticals," she read off the printout. "That's what it says on the boxes in the truck."

"I'll do a search for it," Finn said.

"Did Jordan have any connection to B-Tec?"

Tweety asked.

"Not that I've found," Kat said. "But then again, I haven't found much of anything. It doesn't even seem like she had a job. I spoke with her parents, and they said she left home when she was seventeen." Kat shook her head.

"Her mom said she would call every once in while, but she never asked for any money. She's definitely no trust fund kid. And I asked her mom if Jordan had any sisters, and her mom said, 'No, thank God! One girl is trouble enough.' So, not exactly the Brady Bunch over there."

"Did she say anything else?" Nick asked.

"She said Jordan was so wild, even the nuns couldn't sort her out." Kat picked up one of the pictures of Jordan. "I wonder if she was doing something illegal?"

"Like what?" Tweety asked.

"I have no idea. Take your pick: drugs, prostitution, burglary, blackmail?" Kat said.

"I don't know, Kat. Billy said she was a nice girl. Fun, big dreams, and all that," Nick said.

"Do you still think her roommates are in danger?" Egghead asked.

"Yes, but we can't go to them with anything specific until we have more information about Ben. There is no way they would believe us," Nick said, sitting up.

"They think Billy killed Jordan. And they have no reason to trust us," Finn said.

"It's not just that. Kayla and Ben are together. Somehow he has convinced her that he loves her."

Exhausted, Nick lay his head back down.

"Hopefully, Mugsy will find something on Ben," Tweety said.

"He'd better, because none of this makes any sense," Kat said.

Kat threw down the pages on to the coffee table. Then she picked up the pictures of Kayla.

"This one is Kayla?" she asked, holding up the image to the light.

"Oh, yeah. The superhottie. She answered the door for Bishop in a towel, fresh from a steamy shower," Tweety said.

Kat gave Nick an odd look, but he could not read it. She didn't say anything but went back to looking at the photos. His head hurt. He put the ice back on his face and tried not to imagine Kayla's smoldering eyes or her full lips parting to smile at him. Then he tried not to think about her lying in a pool of her own blood.

They spent the rest of the afternoon passing Kat's laptop around, doing searches for the few clues they had. Finn was printing out information about B-Tec Pharmaceuticals, which was a subsidiary of Symultec Industries, and Kat was staring at the printouts on the table.

Nick's whole body hurt. It felt like he had been run over by car. He closed his eyes, breathing in the Mackenzie house scent: *oatmeal cookies and Murphy's Oil Soap*. He wasn't exactly sure when he fell asleep, but he was vaguely aware of a few blissfully pain-free moments right before he drifted off.

Nick was standing in a long hallway. Door after door lined both walls as far as he could see. The hallway receded into a tiny point somewhere out in infinity. Nothing was familiar; he didn't recognize where he was. He knew he was dreaming because of the odd slowness to his movements, the heaviness of his limbs.

He opened the first door. Kayla was there in a towel, just like the first time he saw her.

"Oh, you're early," she said, smiling. "I'm so glad you're here." She stepped toward him and wrapped her arms around his neck.

"You're so sweet to worry about me."

Nick watched water drip from her hair to her shoulder. He watched the bead of water roll over her skin, but the drip changed color, turning red. Blood was running down her neck and spreading, blossoming onto the white towel like a bright red flower.

When he looked down, his shirt was drenched in blood. He stepped backward and tripped over something: it was Jordan's dead body, just as he remembered it in the trailer, lying in a pool of blood.

The room spun.

The walls of the room were closing in on him.

"Do you have a death wish, kid?"

It was Kayla's voice, but when he looked up, Ben Sherman was standing above him. A gun was tucked into Ben's waistband. Nick tried to run, but he slipped in Jordan's blood. He finally found his footing and was running down the hallway.

A door in front of him opened and Billy was

standing in the doorway. He was wearing the prison-issue orange jumpsuit, his hands were handcuffed, and his ankles were shackled. Metal doors and gates were clinking shut behind him.

"Nick, what are you doing? Don't leave me here!"

The door slammed shut. Nick tried to open the door, but it was locked. Nick looked over his shoulder and Ben was running after him. Nick ran. He tried to run faster, but it felt like he was moving in slow motion. The air around him was thick and syrupy.

Run faster, he thought, but his limbs felt cumbersome. He dragged himself down the hallway, awash with fear and panic. He could see Kat at the end of the hallway. She was filming him with her camera. She smiled and gave him a little finger wave.

When he woke up, it was dark. Rain was pitter-pattering against the windowpanes. Kat was sitting on the arm of the recliner facing him.

"Hey."

"Hey. Where is everybody?" Nick looked around the dark empty living room.

"Egghead had to take off. He dropped the guys off at Tweety's. My mom finally got out of bed. She took one look at your battered face, and some of her maternal instincts reemerged. She went to the grocery store for provisions, but she thought you should rest."

"Did Mugsy call? Did he find anything?" Nick was feeling groggy.

He tried hard to focus his foggy mind.

"No, not yet."

Nick closed his eyes. His face and chest ached. Even his teeth hurt.

"You're face looks better," Kat said.

"It's dark in here. You can't see my face," Nick laughed.

"That explains it," Kat said.

"When my mom gets back, I'll have her call your dad, tell him your sleeping over here tonight. The longer you go without him seeing you like this, the better."

"Good idea."

Then they sat silent in the dark room, listening to the rain come down outside the window. Nick felt like he had a million things to say. He wanted to tell her so many things, but the words just spun around his head, like clothes in the dryer: every thought was soggy and not ready to come out. He tried to think about what words would even come close to expressing what he was feeling.

You are important to me. That sounded corny even in his head. Plus, she knew that. He didn't have to say that.

When I thought I was going to die, I thought of you.

She would laugh at that, he knew.

Kat has no patience for the melodramatic. Then he thought, maybe he didn't need to explain any of it; he could just say what was on top of every confusing thing he was feeling.

Climb into this recliner with me, let me bury my nose in your hair, and let's pretend none of this is actually happening.

"What are you thinking about?" Kat asked.

"Nothing," he said quickly.

"Liar. What are you thinking about?"

"I don't know. Everything." Nick was glad it was dark. "I mean, did you ever think that you could have one kind of life at the beginning of the week, a pretty normal life where your biggest concerns are perfecting your race start and enjoying the summer, and at the end of the week be a totally different person altogether? Because life all of a sudden cracked open, and things you thought only happened on TV and in the movies started happening? It doesn't seem real, and yet there's nowhere to go to escape from it."

"I know, it's crazy. It's like what I saw on the Discovery channel: a shark will sink if it stops swimming. I just want to curl up and hide under the covers, but if I do that, what's going to happen to

Billy? And who's going to take care of my mom?"

"Exactly. It's up to us to figure this out."

"I'm so glad you are here to help." Kat's voice shook a little as she spoke. "If anyone can help Billy, it's you."

Nick's insides flushed with heat. Having Kat believe in him was an intoxicating feeling. The pain of his face and his chest receded to a dull ache. He shook off the residue of his nightmare. He felt awake and ready to get back to work.

"Let's take another look at everything we know."

SATURDAY

By the next morning, Kat and Nick had examined and reexamined every scrap of information they had, and they were no closer to knowing what was going on, or proving Billy's innocence.

"I think we should ride out to the quarry to the spot marked on the map and see what we find," Kat said, pointing to the spot off the Interstate.

"What about your arm? Can you ride?"

"I'll be fine." Kat wriggled her fingers, showing him she could work the throttle and the front brake, despite the cast.

"What about you? Can you ride?" she asked.

Nick stretched his arms above his head. He could feel that his left side was sore and tender, but not too bad. He stepped over to the hallway mirror. A lot of the swelling in his face had gone down, and he could open his left eye fully. The arnica gel Finn's grandfather had given him was working pretty good—better than Nick had expected. The dark purple bruising was gradating into a more greenish color on the side of his face.

Not bad.

"Let's do it. We'll have to ride two-up to Finn's. My bike is still there."

It had stopped raining, but the grass was still wet and the sky was a flat, gloomy gray. Nick swung his leg over the seat and slid behind Kat on her bike. He hadn't ridden on the back of her bike since they were nine years old. That one time, Kat had made him nervous by speeding along a trail while low branches battered their arms and smacked their goggles and faces.

This time, he was nervous for a whole different reason. He wasn't sure how close to get, and he debated where to put his hands. Luckily, Kat motioned for him to move forward in the seat, and once he was right up against her, he reached around her waist and held on.

Kat was a great rider. She skillfully navigated the trail back to Finn's house. Even though the trail was muddy and slippery from the rain the night before, the ride was smooth. Their helmets never bumped, and Kat kept the bike balanced. They pulled up to Finn's house and Nick jumped off.

He missed the feeling of Kat immediately. The cold and damp filled the spots on his arms, legs, and chest that just a second ago were warm from being next to her. Nick went under the deck and rolled his bike out from under the shadows. He kick-started it. Mr. Foley came out on to the deck and saluted them. Nick waved and followed Kat back into the woods.

Kat was obviously having fun being back on her bike. The doctor had told her to lay off riding until her wrist was healed up, but the cast wasn't slowing her down at all. She obviously had missed it. They hit the dirt logging road and she accelerated, pulling a wheelie. They rode along the outer edge of the quarry, through the stench of the municipal dump, cutting west along the north end and making their way to the spot Ben had marked on the map.

The hum of cars and trucks speeding along the Interstate carried through the trees to where Kat and Nick hid their bikes in the woods off the trail. The dirt road butted up against the Interstate at a T, but the entrance was blocked with a chain-link fence and gate.

Kat pointed to the fresh tire tracks in the soft mud. She walked over to the gate.

"It looks like somebody came through here this morning, after it stopped raining. There's a chain, but no padlock." She spoke in a whisper.

"The tracks turn off the road right there." Nick pointed to a clearing in the trees.

Kat came back away from the gate so they could view the tracks from the cover of the woods. They walked through the trees as quietly as they could, following the tracks while still staying hidden. The branches and pine boughs they brushed up against were heavy and dripping from the rain, and by the time Kat and Nick had walked a half mile, they were both soaking wet.

Finally, Nick signaled Kat to stop and he squinted through the trees. There was a building a hundred yards away. He would have missed it if all of the garage doors had been closed, because the color of the building camouflaged so well with the surrounding forest. But luckily, one of the three garage doors was wide open.

Nick and Kat took careful steps forward to get a better look. Inside the open garage door they could see Ben Sherman mixing up paint and pouring it into plastic containers and screwing those to the bottoms of compression-powered paint guns. A plain white tractor-trailer cab was parked in the middle garage bay.

Nick and Kat continued to creep forward until they could see past the cab to where four glittery gold motorcycles were parked. The paint sparkled even in the shadows of the metal building. Nick squinted and could see white wings painted on the tanks.

Kat grabbed the back of his shirt and yanked him to the ground.

"Kat, what are you . . . ?"

"Shh. Listen."

Nick heard the distinct sound of a BMW GS 1200 motor approaching along the road behind them. Nick and Kat lay still on the ground. The damp earth felt cold. The deep rich smell of dirt from the forest floor filled Nick's nostrils. He was surprised by how clean dirt could smell.

The motorcycle passed by them and stopped just outside the garage doors. Nick raised his head a few inches but couldn't see anything. The engine went quiet, and he heard a woman's voice.

"Are we ready?"

"Another hour or so and yeah, we'll be ready," Nick heard Ben say.

"Good. Keep the police scanner on. You'll know when it's time, probably between six and seven," the woman said.

Nick heard the motorcycle engine turn over and then the sound traveled away into the distance, going in a different direction from the way she came.

"The road must continue past the building," Nick whispered.

"There is another logging road a half mile away," Kat whispered back. "It connects with Route 28 north of here."

"The GS is a dual-purpose bike," Nick said. "It can go from the mud to the street. It can easily go along any of the dirt trails around here."

Nick and Kat lay silent on the ground until they heard the squeal and hum of the compressor in the building. They slowly rose up off the ground, onto their hands and knees. Ben had his back to them.

Staying crouched, Nick and Kat quickly and quietly snuck away. Once they were out of sight, they ran back to their bikes.

"What is going on?" Kat asked, still whispering, when they got back to their bikes. "What are they doing?"

"I have no idea, but let's get out of here. Are you okay?"

Kat nodded and put on her helmet. As they rode back to Kat's house, a light rain began to fall. Nick felt each drop on his skin like an icy little stab.

"The hot golden motorcycle chick?" Tweety asked. "What's her connection to Ben?"

"I'm not sure, but I think she's the boss of whatever scheme they are planning. Maybe she's the same woman from the Breeze Inn the other night," Nick said.

He had traded his soaking wet clothes for a pair of Billy's pants and one of his T-shirts. The clothes hung loose on Nick's smaller frame. Now dry and back in the Mackenzie living room, Nick was doing a new search on the computer.

Kat had called Tweety and Finn as soon as they got back to the house, and they arrived soon after. Nick told them everything about the garage they found on the dirt road off the Interstate.

"So, what are you searching for?" Finn asked.

"Greta, the lady from Slim's, mentioned that this guy stole a truck full of prescription drugs, probably being delivered from where they make the pills to pharmacies."

Nick handed a few sheets of paper to Finn.

"I thought she was just gossiping, so I didn't think too much about it. But I think it is important."

"On their website Symultec Industries lists their manufacturing facilities, B-Tec pharmaceuticals, in Silver City, New Mexico. That means that to ship to pharmacies in Colorado, Wyoming, Montana, and even Canada, it's a straight shot up the Interstate. An article I found about the truck driver, this guy Gus Farley, said he was last seen headed north from New Mexico. Then he and his truck just vanished after crossing the state line." Nick showed them the map on the screen.

"When was this?" Tweety asked.

"About a month ago," Nick said.

"Right around the time Ben came to town."
Tweety sunk down on to the couch.

"Maybe now we can take this to the police," Finn
said.

"We don't have anything except suspicion," Nick
said.

"We have the pictures."

"Which I broke into Ben's room to get. They
would just throw me in jail with Billy." Nick sighed.
"No, we have to go there tonight and find out exactly
what's going on. And we need to find out who the
golden rider is."

"How does any of this involve Billy?" Kat got up
and was standing over the coffee table. She looked
agitated. And Nick completely understood. It felt like
they were so close to grasping what was right in front
of them, but for now they were coming up empty-
handed.

"Hopefully, that's what we'll find out tonight."
Nick pulled out a map of the area and marked the
intersection of the logging road and Route 28.

"Tweety, you will be here. If a truck or a
motorcycle comes out of the woods and onto Route
28, get the license plate number and call the police."

"What do I say? That I think they have a
truckload of stolen drugs?" Tweety sounded
incredulous. "They'll think it's a prank."

"Tell them that they are driving recklessly,
swerving all over the road, and you think they are
drunk," Kat said.

Tweety thought it over and then nodded, satisfied.

"Finn, you are going to do the same thing, except you will be here, at the intersection with the Interstate. You will have to walk through the woods to get into place, and once you're there, stay out of sight."

Nick lowered his voice to a whisper.

"Ben and that chick at the Breeze Inn were armed the last time we saw them. I think it is safe to assume they will be again."

He eyed the ceiling in the direction of Mrs. Mackenzie's room, where she was lying down. They all looked in that direction and listened. No movement, not a sound. A shadow of sadness crossed over Kat's face, but then it passed. She was looking intently at the map.

"And we'll be here, at the edge of the building," Kat said.

Nick stood up and started gathering up the papers on the coffee table. Mrs. Mackenzie did occasionally emerge from her room, and Nick didn't think she needed to see any of this lying around. Then Tweety's cell phone rang. He checked the screen and flipped his phone open.

"Mugs! What's the good news?" Tweety listened to his brother on the other end of the line. His face fell, and he shook his head at Nick.

"Okay. Yeah. Let us know." Tweety closed his phone. "Mugs said he didn't find a criminal record for any of the prints we sent, but he is expanding the search into other databases."

Nick nodded.

"We should get going. We want to be in place

before six, if we can."

Nick and Kat followed the same route they had earlier in the day to the grayish-brown metal building. The sun was low in the sky but still above the tree line. They were very careful as they crept through the woods, keeping their ears open for approaching vehicles. They only thing they heard was the distant hum of rush-hour traffic on the Interstate.

The three garage doors were closed, and Nick did not see any cars or motorcycles on this side of the building. He and Kat inched closer. They were about twenty feet away when the garage door at the far end of the building began to open. Nick and Kat dove to the ground, hiding behind a thicket.

Nick could see a little through the branches. He saw a blue compact car pull out of the building and drive down the dirt road toward the Interstate. A pretty girl Nick recognized from Ben's stalker photos was driving the car.

Nick and Kat did not dare speak as more activity began in the building. They lay as still as they could in the dirt and watched the events unfold. The other two doors opened, and a gold motorcycle followed the blue car. Nick could hear Ben bark orders, and another gold motorcycle peeled out of the building, speeding away down the dirt road. The GS is the perfect bike to take from the street to a muddy little dirt road like this one. *It could handle even tougher terrain,* Nick thought.

The riders were all women and they were wearing gold riding gear, with praying hands in a circle of roses on the backs of their jackets, just like the woman they saw at the track the day Jordan was murdered.

Everything was quiet except for the hum of the traffic and the murmur of a police scanner Ben had on inside the building. Nick and Kat lay on the ground listening for almost an hour. Nick's arm started to fall asleep.

An explosion echoed in the distance. It was quiet for a few minutes. Then they heard Ben inside.

"This is it!" He turned up the scratchy police scanner, and Nick could hear it echo through the metal building.

"This is car 45, over." Static crinkled loudly.

"Go ahead, 45, over."

"We've got a code 3, an 11-25, and a possible 11-83. A car is on fire right in the middle of the highway, and I can't see if there is anybody in it."

The voice on the radio was urgent. "Request a 10-49 and all available cars. I repeat, all available cars, mile marker 82 on the Interstate, the northbound lane, over."

Ben turned the police scanner volume down to murmur. There were sirens screaming somewhere beyond the woods. Kat and Nick exchanged looks, but Nick shrugged. He had no idea what any of that meant. Then he heard the sound of a motorcycle engine, and one of the gold BMWs roared toward the building.

A huge semi looked impossibly big following the bike down the small dirt road. Nick could see as the eighteen-wheeler pulled up to the middle garage bay opening that it had "Symultec Industries" painted on the side of the cab.

The passenger door of the cab opened and the

limp body of a man rolled out. Ben dragged the body inside the building.

"Is he dead?" Kat whispered.

Nick watched the body disappear into the first garage bay. The man's Timberland work boots dragged across the concrete floor.

He sure looks dead, Nick thought, but only shrugged again at Kat. He reached out and took her hand in his.

Ben ran around the semi disconnecting the tractor cab from its load. He drove the disconnected cab into the first garage bay and backed the plain white tractor up to the Symultec Industries trailer.

Gabby appeared and replaced the license plate and the mud flaps on the back of the truck. Ben drove the semi into the garage, and he and Gabby started spraying the whole trailer with white paint.

It was incredible how quickly the eighteen-wheeler was transformed. The compressed-air paint sprayers covered four-foot swaths in seconds, and both sides were complete in less than five minutes. Gabby jumped into the cab and drove out the other side of the building, just as one of the gold motorcycles drove up and followed the truck in the direction of Route 28.

Ben was closing up the garage bays when a third gold GS came down the dirt road. Ben said something, but Nick couldn't hear it over the idling motor. Nick strained his neck watching, trying to see what was happening. The rider pulled a gun from inside her gold jacket and fired three rounds into Ben's chest.

Kat and Nick flattened themselves to the ground. Kat's eyes were round and Nick could see the fear in them. She was squeezing his hand hard, the silent equivalent, Nick realized, of screaming. The GS tore away into the night, leaving Nick and Kat staring at each other, frozen in disbelief.

"Stay here, and call an ambulance. And call Tweety and Finn so they can flag down the paramedics and get them back here through the woods!"

Nick jumped up and ran over to Ben. There was blood on his right shoulder and arm. Ben's chest was covered in blood. Nick pressed his two fingers to Ben's neck under his jaw. Nick felt a pulse, but blood was quickly pooling around Ben's body.

"Explain to me again exactly what you kids were doing there." Officer Tucker was eyeing them suspiciously.

They were sitting in the waiting room at West Central Memorial Hospital. Kat, Nick, Tweety, and Finn were sitting in a row on the hard plastic bucket seats.

"Officer, we were just dirt riding in the woods. All of a sudden there were motorcycles and a semi and gunshots, and we called the police right away," Tweety said in his most genuine tone, with an innocent, angelic look to match.

"Officer Tucker?" A young woman doctor interrupted them. "He's out of surgery. He's still unconscious, but he's stable."

Officer Tucker scowled at Tweety. "Wait here. Don't move." And he walked away toward a cluster of other police officers and doctors.

Tweety and Nick exchanged looks.

"He doesn't believe us," Nick said.

Tweety shrugged. "That's my story, and I'm sticking to it." Tweety's phone rang and he flipped it open.

"Hey, Mugs." Tweety listened to his brother on the phone. "Are you kidding me?"

He hit Nick in the side with the back of his hand, and Nick cringed with pain. Tweety had smacked him right on his bruised rib.

"Are you absolutely sure?" Tweety asked. He mouthed "Sorry" to Nick, as Nick rubbed his side.

"I'll fill you in later, Mugs. Thanks a lot." Tweety flipped his phone closed and whispered in a low voice to his friends, "That hacker buddy of Mugs found Ben's prints in a federal database."

"Federal prison?" Kat asked in a whisper.

"No. Federal payroll."

Nick and Kat and Finn sat silently staring at Tweety.

"FBI, guys! Undercover FBI!" Tweety raised his voice more than he meant to, but only a nurse seemed to notice. She glared at them and then disappeared into the nurses' station.

"Ben is an FBI agent?" Finn stared, flabbergasted.

SUNDAY

This was torturous for Nick. He was under strict orders from his father and Officer Tucker to stay home and out of trouble.

"Let the police sort this out," his father pleaded.

Nick was reading the paper in the morning, and then spent the afternoon on the phone with Kat and Tweety and Finn. Trying to puzzle together the pieces.

Shipment of Pharmaceutical Drugs Stolen in Highway Robbery

JULY 1 – WEST CENTRAL, Colo. (AP) – According to police, a car fire on the Interstate was a distraction for a pharmaceutical drug heist Saturday evening.

Police said a gang of thieves blocked the Interstate with a car and hijacked an eighteen-wheeler, which contained a pharmaceutical shipment of Oxycontin, around 6 p.m. They set fire to the empty car to block the road and aid their escape.

Investigators say the same gang may have been involved in a similar robbery a month ago.

Police say one suspect drove the tractor-trailer northbound on the Interstate, while the burning car distracted police and rescue crews. The tractor-trailer was driven off the highway onto an unmarked road, where the gang changed the appearance of the truck to elude detection.

At 7:45 p.m. police received a 911 call reporting a gunshot injury. The injured man was discovered by a group of teenagers, who happened upon the thieves in the middle of the heist.

"We were just dirt riding in the woods. All of a sudden there were motorcycles and a semi and gunshots, and we called the police right away," said Lewis Emmit Clark, 16.

The police haven't yet released the name of the gunshot victim, and it is unclear if the man was involved in the robbery. The truck driver, Stephen Samuel Riley, 46, was found unconscious at the scene. Both of the injured men are recovering at West Central Memorial Hospital.

Anonymous phone calls reported suspicious activity and reckless driving, as the truck and motorcycles detoured onto a smaller county road. However, the stolen vehicle evaded apprehension, while police and emergency services dealt with the vehicle fire and resulting traffic on the Interstate.

"We wouldn't have even known the truck had been stolen until days later, if there hadn't been witnesses. Unfortunately, all the details were not given at the time of the 911 calls. Chasing after a truck could not be made a priority when there was a gunshot wound and many innocent people still in harm's way," said Officer Jack Tenely.

All members of the gang eluded police Saturday.

Police say they have recovered the tractor-trailer, which was found abandoned on the side of a small dirt road. All of the stolen pharmaceutical drugs had been removed at some point after the robbery.

"They didn't make it a priority?" Kat said with disgust.

Nick could hear her crinkling the newspaper on the other line.

"We didn't give them enough details," Nick said, switching his phone to the other ear. "We should have called the police earlier."

"This is not our fault, Nick! How in the world were we supposed to know anyone would get hurt?"

MONDAY

Robbery Highlights Rampant Spread of Drug Abuse

JULY 2 – Associated Press – Oxycontin abuse is on the rise, especially in poor rural areas like West Central, Colorado, the location of a dramatic heist Saturday of a truck full of pharmaceutical painkillers.

The abuse of Oxycontin is rampant for several reasons. The elevated opiate dosage makes it highly addictive. Oxycontin is covered by most health insurance plans, so it is significantly cheaper than street drugs.

In addition, the dosage of an Oxycontin pill is consistent, unlike drugs such as cocaine or heroin that can be laced with other substances.

Oxycontin is prescribed to cancer patients as an alternative to morphine. The drug is highly addictive, expensive, and can be lethal. Many rural states have declared Oxycontin abuse an epidemic. Oxycontin is referred to as "hillbilly heroin" or "the poor man's heroin."

"It's just terrible. We've seen the effects right here in town, and the effects are just devastating. How it just pulls lives apart. Honestly, it's just terrible," said Greta Stapleton, a resident of West Central and a local business owner.

No one from Symultec Industries, the producers of Oxycontin, was available for comment at the time of this article.

Nick's phone rang, buzzing on the kitchen table next to his empty cereal bowl and the spread out paper. He flipped it open.

"Are they calling us hillbillies?" Finn asked.

Nick dialed Kat's number.

"Hey, what's up?" Kat said on the other line.

"Do you think your mom would mind coming to pick me up on the way to visit Billy?"

"I thought your dad didn't want you leaving the house."

"Like he'd notice," Nick said more to himself than to Kat.

"What? You're breaking up. Say that again."

"He's not here, and besides, I'd be with your mom. I'm sure it's fine."

"Okay. We'll come by in an hour."

Nick snapped shut his phone. He reread the newspaper article, and wracked his brain about what any of this had to do with Billy.

Visiting hours at the county facility were very strict: one to three on Monday afternoons. Nick, Kat, and Mrs. Mackenzie arrived at the county jail at exactly one o'clock, but there were other people already there waiting to get in. They went through the metal detectors one at a time, and the guards buzzed them through the series of gates that led to the yellow visiting room.

They followed an older woman and her grandson into the room. The pair chose the table farthest to the right, and the grandmother pulled coloring books and crayons out of her bag for the young boy. Nick followed Mrs. Mackenzie and Kat to the center table and waited.

A guard brought in a young man, maybe a few years older than Billy, through the gates into the visiting area. He sat with the older woman and the kid. Nick could hear some of what they were saying, and it was all incredibly benign.

"Sherry is going to drive the school bus again next year. She keeps saying she's going to retire, but you know her. She just likes to complain," the woman was telling the young man in the orange jumpsuit.

Nick was feeling less anxious this time, but he wondered if he could ever feel like it was normal. He tried to imagine what it would be like if Billy stayed in here, living but not living, getting old but missing life. Could Nick come here every Monday and give him recaps of the race weekends? It would be beyond depressing. He shuddered with the thought of it.

The gates opened and the guard escorted Billy in. He held his hands out while the guard uncuffed him. Mrs. Mackenzie was doing better today. She didn't start sobbing. She seemed to be holding her breath.

At least she's holding it together, Nick thought.

Billy sat down.

"Are you al right?" Mrs. Mackenzie asked as she grabbed up his hands in hers.

"I'm fine."

"Do you need anything?"

"I'm fine, Mom."

Nick thought that was a ridiculous thing to keep saying under the circumstances.

"Mr. Kratchner is going to meet us here," Kat said.

"Did he find new evidence?" Billy asked.

"He didn't say."

They sat in silence, looking at the grooves in the surface of the table.

"Did you hear about the robbery?" Nick asked.

"Yeah. It's crazy. I saw Tweety in the newspaper," Billy said. He almost smiled.

"Did you know anything about it?" Kat asked.

"How would I?" Billy narrowed his eyes at his sister.

"She means, in retrospect, is there anything about the robbery that rings any bells?" Nick asked.

"No. I don't know anything about it." Billy looked past Nick.

Nick turned around and waddling sideways to squeeze through the metal gates was Mr. Kratchner. An overstuffed briefcase dangled from his right hand and under his other arm he carried a messy stack of papers and manila folders.

He spotted the Mackenzies and Nick. He lifted his left hand awkwardly in acknowledgement and the stack under his arm came loose and fell. The paper cascade landed on the floor in a fan pattern.

"Oh, my! Oh, dear," Mr. Kratchner said, but he made no attempt to retrieve the papers. Instead, he walked over to the table and heaved his bulging briefcase onto the table with a thud. Nick jumped up and pushed the papers as neatly as he could back into a stack and brought the pile over to where Mr. Kratchner had settled himself at the table with the Mackenzies.

"Many thanks, Mr. Bishop. You are too kind." They waited, staring, while Mr. Kratchner caught his breath and wiped his forehead with a handkerchief.

"Sorry I'm late. I had to get copies of the case reports from the district attorney, and it's like pulling teeth. I told him I'd come over and photocopy them myself, if that was the hold up." Mr. Kratcher sighed and tucked his handkerchief back in his pocket.

"Not *me* literally, but I'd send Melissa," he explained.

"Is there good news in that stack of papers?" Kat asked.

"Well, yes. In a way there is."

"Really?" Mrs. Mackenzie was holding on to Billy's hands so tightly Nick could see the white impressions she was causing in his skin. "What is it?"

"Well, the report finds that there are no eyewitnesses who saw William kill Miss Graham." Mr. Kratchner smiled pleasantly.

"I didn't kill her," Billy said.

"What did or did not actually happen does not matter as much as the facts I can present at trial."

Nick and the Mackenzies stared at him in stunned silence.

"And this is good?" Mrs. Mackenzie finally asked.

"Well, it would be a lot worse if there *was* an eyewitness who was going to testify that they saw William kill Miss Graham."

"Is that all?" Kat had shrunk down a little on the aluminum bench.

"No! There's more!" Mr. Kratchner excitedly grabbed one of the manila folders from the stack and opened it on the table. "The lab results came back. The murder weapon and the entrance of the trailer were both wiped clean of prints!"

"Won't they just say I wiped them?" Billy's face was twisted into a grimace of confusion.

Nick felt the same way.

How was this good?

"And! They tested all of your race gear from your duffel bag. No trace of blood was found at all." Mr. Kratchner was smiling from ear to ear.

"I could have told you that," Billy said, eyeing Kratchner wearily.

"But this"—Kratchner waved the lab report in the air—"I can present in court! This is evidence."

"It sounds more like lack of evidence," Nick said.

"Ah, very astute, Mr. Bishop. That is true. But it is the prosecutor's burden to produce evidence that Mr. Mackenzie is guilty. And so lack of evidence is good news for us."

That didn't make sense. Nick didn't feel at all reassured.

"Time's up." The far gate clanged open as the guard entered the room. Billy stood. Mrs. Mackenzie stood too and held on to Billy's hands.

"Ma'am, please," the guard said.

Mrs. Mackenzie nodded. She kissed Billy's hands and then finally let go. Tears streamed down her face as the guard put handcuffs on Billy's wrists, and as he escorted Billy through the gates, Mrs. Mackenzie's sobs bounced off the aluminum tables and filled the yellow room with their vibrating echoes.

Mrs. Mackenzie angled the station wagon into Nick's driveway. Nick slid off the bench seat and out the passenger-side door.

"Nick?" Mrs. Mackenzie said.

He leaned down and looked back into the car. Kat and her mom had both been crying on the ride home. Nick had never thought they looked anything alike. Mrs. Mackenzie dyed her hair blond, and she was always reapplying coats of bright red lipstick. But today, sitting next to each other, Nick could see they held their bodies the same way, and their bloodshot eyes were the same shape.

"Thank you," Mrs. Mackenzie said. "There are people in this town who are treating me and Kat like we have something contagious. And it's just . . . well, thank you."

"Of course," Nick said. He paused, but then he just held his hand up as a good-bye. He closed the door and watched them drive away.

When Nick walked into the kitchen, his dad was on the phone, running his fingers through his thinning hair. His father had said even less than usual to him over the past couple days—ever since Officer Tucker had dropped him off at home Saturday night. Tucker had told his dad his theory that Nick and his friends were not there by accident.

"Randy, it does not bode well for your son that he is mixed up with three major criminal investigations, including robbery, attempted murder, and murder. Two murders!"

Tucker had glared at Nick, and then he softened to speak to Nick's father. "In less than a week he has found himself more than his share of trouble. He won't say who pummeled his face. He says no one, but considering what he's mixed up in, I don't believe him. I don't know exactly how he's involved, but I recommend you don't let him out of your sight until all of this has blown over. Because I swear, if I find him at one more crime scene, I'm going to have to arrest him for tampering with evidence, interfering with a police investigation, hindering prosecution, and anything else I can think of."

Nick's father had said nothing. He'd nodded and stared at the floor. At the time, Nick wondered why he hadn't said anything in his defense, like "My son is a good kid. I'm sure this is all a mistake," but he hadn't said a thing. He had wordlessly walked Officer Tucker to the door, and he hadn't said very much since.

Now, standing in the kitchen, awash with afternoon sunlight, Randy Bishop had dark purple circles under his eyes. His shoulders were slumped and his hair was sticking up in different directions. He had been a shadow of himself ever since Nick's mom had walked out, but now he looked even more vacant, if that were possible. He hung up the phone and turned around to where Nick was standing in the doorway.

"Where have you been?" His dad's voice was low but full of barely contained anger.

"I went to see Billy."

"What did I say to you? You were supposed to stay home. I don't want you in the middle of this trouble! This is all very dangerous. You are covered in bruises from who-knows-what!"

"Dad, I fell! I swear, I'm telling the truth!"

"This is not a game! This is serious. You have no idea what Billy is involved with. Two girls are dead! The FBI is investigating, for Christ's sake!"

Nick didn't say anything. Watching his father yell was like watching an actor play Randy Bishop on TV. His dad had been such a zombie the past four years. Nick didn't know how to respond. His dad was stiff and out of practice from not showing any emotion at all for so long. Nick almost laughed at him.

"You can't tie yourself to someone else's problems," Nick's dad continued. "It will pull you down like a sinking anchor."

You can't be serious, Nick thought.

His head surged with a bolt of rage. Nick gripped the kitchen counter and bowed his head, bracing himself while the wave of anger crashed in his brain. The ensuing floodwaters broke loose bits and pieces of anger that had calcified over the years. Disappointments he thought he didn't care about. Silences he thought didn't matter. They came to the surface and overflowed out of him.

"You're such a hypocrite! You are the king of lost causes, and you're lecturing *me* on how I need to distance myself from other people's problems?"

He wanted to hit something or throw something.

"Mom was a sinking anchor and you didn't distance yourself from *her*! You held on to her to the very end. You're pathetic! You are *still* holding on!"

Nick felt as though his thoughts were rushing out of his mouth through some sort of emergency release valve. It was wide open and there was no turning it off. "You know who you have distanced yourself from? Me! I've been all by myself for the last four years . . . actually, no! Longer than that, because it was worse when she was here, and now . . . *now* you're going to tell me that I need to give up on the person who was there for me when you weren't!"

"You don't have the right," Nick finished, feeling suddenly mean and empty.

His father stood still staring at Nick as if he were trying to catch his breath. His eyes were glassy and Nick had a sinking feeling his dad was going to cry. He really did not want to see his dad cry. Even worse, he didn't want to be the one to make his dad cry.

Nick stood frozen. The telephone on the kitchen wall rang. Neither of them moved. The phone rang again and Randy Bishop took a deep breath. He turned away from his son and answered the phone.

Serves him right, Nick thought half-heartedly. He was still mad, but now concern was melting the anger. Nick had hit his dad with a battering ram. He had been so careful with his father all this time, and now he felt weirdly like a bully.

"Yes, of course," Nick's dad was saying into the phone. "Right now? Yes. That's fine." Nick's dad hung up the receiver but kept his back turned.

"Who was that?" Nick asked.

Randy Bishop ran his hands through his hair and leaned up against the counter.

"That was Agent Diaz from the FBI. He would like you to come to the hospital. He has a few questions for you." His voice was even. Was he angry? Hurt? Ashamed? Or numb as usual? Nick couldn't tell.

They rode to the hospital in total silence. His dad

stared straight ahead as he drove. The world felt off-balance. Nick was disturbed by the fact that his dad didn't yell back at him, but relieved that he did not break down weeping. Nick kept trying to think of something to say, but the floodgates that had opened earlier were now locked down. He couldn't get words to come out of his mouth no matter how hard he tried.

They arrived at the hospital and were met by a dark-suited federal agent. The agent escorted them up to the fourth floor, through a handful of police and other federal agents, to a private room where Special Agent Diaz was waiting. Ben Sherman was lying in a hospital bed. He had tubes hooked up to IVs in his arm, and there were machines flashing and blipping behind his bed.

"Nick, thanks for coming. I'd like to introduce you to Special Agent Ben Shapiro." Special Agent Diaz slapped a heavy hand on Nick's back.

Ben nodded slightly.

"Hi," Nick said, and lifted his hand in a weak wave.

"Mr. Bishop," Diaz said, "Agent Shapiro would like a few minutes to speak with your son, alone."

"Is he in trouble? Do I need to get him a lawyer?" Nick's dad defensively stepped between Agent Diaz and Nick. *Well, that's new*, Nick thought, trying to remember the last time his father had stood up for him.

"No, not at all," Agent Diaz said. "The Bureau's official stance is that your son and his friends were at the scene by happenstance, and it's lucky for Agent Shapiro they were."

Diaz leaned into Mr. Bishop and whispered, "I

think he wants to thank Nick for saving his life."

"Oh." Rabdy Bishop's eyes widened, and he nodded at Shapiro in the bed. Then awkwardly backed out of the room. Diaz followed him and closed the door behind them.

"You don't have to thank me . . . ," Nick started.

"I'm not," Ben interrupted. "Kid, you ruined my investigation! Three months of work and a month undercover, and we still don't know where the drugs were headed. We only got a glimpse at the whole operation."

Shapiro shook his head in disgust. "I told you to stay away, and you just kept sticking your nose in it. The fact that you got an ambulance to me in time to save my life is the only reason I didn't find something serious to charge you with."

"Like what? What did I do?"

"I'm not totally sure what you are involved in, but I have my suspicions. Every time I turned around, you were there! I'd start by charging you with hindering a federal investigation, and see if I found anything that linked you to the robberies."

"I didn't have anything to do with the robbery! I was trying to help my friend."

"Who—Kayla?"

"No," Nick shot back, maybe a little too forcefully. Nick was struck with fear. The FBI might arrest him after all, if they knew he'd broken into Ben's room.

"Billy, my friend who was arrested. Besides, I thought you were a psycho-druggie!"

"I was undercover, kid. It means I go under-a-cover! A disguise. I act like some one I'm not. What part of undercover do you not understand?"

"And I thought you killed Jordan!"

Ben glared at Nick. He spoke through clenched teeth. "What in the world would give you that impression?"

He sat up but cringed with pain, grasping his shoulder and easing back down. He looked at Nick and narrowed his eyes at him.

"And how was it that you and your friends ended up in the woods at the exact time of the robbery?"

Nick bit his lip. There was no way he was going to confess to this federal agent that he had broken into his hotel room and seen surveillance photographs and maps that led him to the metal building off the Interstate.

"We were just dirt riding. We ride up there all the time." Nick shrugged.

"I don't believe you."

Ben looked pale and gaunt and very tired. He eyed Nick for a few seconds.

"Lucky for you, my boss doesn't want the headlines to read 'FBI Investigation Derailed by Pesky Kids,' so for now you are off the hook."

"What did Jordan have to do with all of this?" Nick asked, changing the subject.

"She was a member of the motorcycle gang pulling the drug heist—the Sisters of Mercy," Ben said.

"Really? So who killed her?"

"Kid, I have no idea."

Agent Shapiro looked exhausted, and he grimaced as he shifted in bed and closed his eyes.

"Plenty of evidence points to your friend, the one

they arrested."

Nick felt sick to his stomach. When he first heard the FBI was involved, he had felt sure that they would have other leads pointing to Jordan's real killer. Now he felt deflated.

"Have you spoken to Jordan's roommate, Kayla? Is she all right?" Nick asked.

Ben's eyes shot open and he looked at Nick like he was the dumbest person he had ever met.

"Kid, Kayla's the one who shot me!"

"So Kayla is the leader of a motorcycle gang, a band of thieves, and possibly a major drug ring?"

Tweety shook his head in disbelief. He had snuck out of his house and ridden over after Nick called him. The two of them were sitting on Nick's front porch watching the late afternoon sun silhouette the trees in the west.

"Yeah, and here I thought she was in danger, and needed our protection! And it ends up I probably got a federal agent shot!" Nick felt sick to his stomach.

"Don't worry, Bishop, my lips are sealed."

"I just feel so stupid. I couldn't have made a bigger mess of this. I'm sure I tipped her off in some way with my suspicion of Ben."

"We are searching for truth and justice, my friend. It's a messy business."

Tweety sighed.

"Besides, you didn't give her the surveillance photo. You told her you were worried about her. That's it. How could she extrapolate that Ben was undercover from that? Maybe she already knew? Maybe she didn't know but was planning on killing 'Ben Sherman' to keep his cut of the score? The truth is, you don't know. None of us do."

"I am just as guilty as stupid Tucker for only seeing what I wanted to see." Nick slouched down and put his head in his hands. "I thought she was this innocent girl, and she's really a killer. She was there the day Jordan was killed, remember!"

"It could have been any one of the Sisters of Mercy that day. I seriously think you need to lighten up. We are dealing with crimes that not even the FBI can figure out. We may never know how all the pieces fit together."

"I just feel like an idiot," Nick said.

"Stop beating yourself up about it. We need to focus on helping Billy."

"What can we do now?" Nick felt pretty hopeless.

"We refocus on how to prove he didn't kill Jordan. We brought everything we know to Kratchner, and hopefully he can use it in Billy's defense—alternate theory of the crime and all that."

Tweety shrugged.

"It doesn't seem fair. Kat said the lawyer is expensive. Her mom is going to try to get a second mortgage on their house to pay for it all."

"It's all we can do at this point." Tweety got up and stretched. "I've got to get back. I left a movie on in my room with my door closed, but once its over and quiet, my mom will be on the prowl."

TUESDAY

Gang of Girl Bikers Were under Investigation, Feds Say

JULY 3 – Associated Press – The gang of thieves on motorcycles suspected in Saturday's highway robbery were being investigated, according to federal authorities.

"Investigations into a West Coast drug ring led us to a series of pharmaceutical drug heists. We followed the trail from Utah to New Mexico, and finally here to Colorado. The evidence led to a group of young female bikers who call themselves the Sisters of Mercy," said Special Agent Robert Diaz of the FBI.

The suspects, whose names have not been released yet, are members of the Sisters of Mercy motorcycle gang and are wanted for their alleged participation in the robbery, according to Diaz.

Agent Diaz would not comment on the scope or nature of the investigation, saying the Bureau wasn't releasing further details.

An unnamed source at the West Central Police Department confirmed that the gunshot victim found in the woods off the Interstate was an undercover FBI agent investigating the drug ring.

"The FBI agent was there to put a tracker on the truck and see where else the drugs would lead the Feds. He made no attempt to stop the robbery. And they didn't give local police any kind of heads-up, and that's how people get hurt," said the individual, who was not authorized to speak publicly.

"How much do you want to bet their 'unnamed source' is Tucker?" Tweety asked. Nick could hear Tweety eating on the other end of the line.

"It sounds like him, doesn't it?" Nick switched his phone to the other ear while he scanned the article.

"First it's our fault, now it's the FBI's fault? I think it sounds exactly like Tucker. Not following protocol . . . blah, blah, blah." Tweety's impression of Tucker was pretty dead-on.

"I just wish we had proof that Kayla or one of the other gang members killed Jordan," Nick said.

"I know," Tweety said. "I mean, in theory, I love the idea of smokin' hot Catholic school girls who turn into a badass motorcycle gang of thieves. If that were a comic book, I'd read it."

"Finn thought TV movie."

"No way. It can be turned into a movie after it's a comic book. There is a proper order to these things. It's a progression that allows the characters to get hotter and sassier through each medium, as it gets farther and farther away from the true story and real life."

"You've given this some thought."

"Of course. It's serious business." Tweety didn't sound serious. He was trying to cheer Nick up. But Nick couldn't shake the idea that he could have prevented some of this from happening if they had gone to the police earlier or if they had just given more information to the 911 operator. Nick felt responsible for an FBI agent getting shot.

And the Sisters of Mercy got away. They have their freedom, while Billy is stuck in a six-by-six cell.

Later that afternoon, Nick still felt horrible. He felt stupid and foolish in every possible way. He was sure he had figured out so much, and in reality he had missed what was right in front of him. Mr. Bishop came out on to the front porch and sat stiffly on the steps next to Nick.

"I've been thinking," he said. "What I said to you before about not getting in the middle of Billy's problems."

"Dad," Nick interrupted. "I do not need this right now."

Mr. Bishop put his hand out. "Just let me finish," he said.

Nick normally would have argued but he was tired, and he felt so guilty and stupid already, it wouldn't make much of a difference if his dad piled on a few more things for him to feel bad about: making him worry, putting himself in danger, getting involved in a situation that was way over his head. He knew the basic outline of the speech his dad was going to launch into.

"I've never worried about you before." His dad cleared his throat.

No shit. You've barely noticed me, Nick thought.

"You are strong in a way most people are not. But all of this"—Randy Bishop motioned out toward the horizon—"dead girls and drugs. All of a sudden, I am terrified for you."

"I'm surprised you noticed," Nick said.

It was an unnecessary dig. But Nick felt like there might be an apology coming and he was feeling spiteful. He wasn't sure if he was ready to forgive his dad. He wasn't going to stop helping Billy, and if his dad couldn't see how important it was to him, then screw him.

"I haven't been perfect. I get that. But why didn't you . . ." Nick's dad ran his hands through his hair and sighed. "Why didn't you ever *say* anything?"

"Like what?"

"I don't know. How you felt."

Nick shrugged. He couldn't explain.

"I told you that people are not always what you think they are, and that's true. Sometimes people disappoint you." Nick's dad stared out at the treetops swaying in the breeze. "And sometimes *you* may disappoint other people. I haven't met anybody yet who's perfect. I don't think a person like that exists. Somebody who never makes mistakes and always does the perfect thing."

He took a deep breath and expelled it, running his hands through his hair. "But you and I need to be very clear. I did not give up my right to be your father!" Nick's dad said. "I've been here the whole time. I have worked my ass off to keep a roof over your head and food on the table." Randy Bishop let out another loud sigh and continued more softly. "We don't have a lot, but I made sure you could ride motocross. That, at least, seemed to make you happy."

"It did. It does," Nick said.

"And if you wanted something else … I'm not a mind reader, Nick."

They sat in silence for a long time. Nick knew he had to say something, but he was having trouble picking just one thought out of the dozens that were swimming in his head.

"I just wanted you to be less out of it."

Nick's dad nodded his head. He was looking straight ahead, but Nick thought he could see tears welling up.

"I don't know what to say. I got my heart broken." The tears threatened to overflow, but Randy Bishop blinked them back.

"So, get over it already," Nick said gently.

Nick's dad rolled his eyes and half laughed.

He nodded. "You got it."

They both stared out into the dusk.

Nick climbed into bed that night feeling slightly lighter. The gulf of silence between him and his father had been weighing on him more than he realized. He thought about what his dad said: "And sometimes *you* may disappoint other people." Nick knew all about that, and it helped him forgive his dad a little.

Staring up at the shadows cast on his ceiling, Nick's thoughts turned toward Billy and the investigation. He tried to think of anything else he had missed. He went through a checklist of people and motives and possibilities. His gut told him that the Sisters of Mercy were somehow the key to Billy's freedom. He had seen Kayla shoot Ben with his own eyes.

Nick could hear the breeze rustle the trees beyond his window. Everything outside was backlit by the waning moon. On his ceiling, the shadow shapes of branches and leaves swayed softly. His eyes felt so heavy . . .

Nick was riding his bike along a wooded trail. He accelerated up a dirt ramp, hitting the jump and flying through the air. Time was moving very slowly. Nick stayed suspended in midair as long seconds stretched out in front of him. Gravity had no effect on him. It was a pleasant feeling, floating on his bike twelve feet above the forest floor.

Then he heard another motor. He turned in his seat and he saw Kat racing along the trail. Her suspension compressed all the way down as she landed a jump, blasting through the trees at full speed. Nick was laughing.

"Kat! Kat! I'm up here."

This is so funny, he thought. *She doesn't even see me.*

She passed below him. Then he heard the sound of another motor. He turned back to look. The gold BMW GS exploded from the woods. The gold rider was crouched down behind her handlebars, and the bike blew through the trees at an alarming speed. Nick was floating above the scene, and without realizing it, he was floating higher and higher into the air, farther and farther from the ground below.

"Kat! Watch out! She's behind you!" Nick shouted.

He screamed as loud as he could, but he was so high in the air, the woods below appeared like a miniature model. Two tiny specs moving across the landscape, with the glittering gold spot closing in on the spot Nick knew was Kat. Gunshots echoed below, and without warning, gravity returned with full force.

The bike was ripped from his grip. Nick was falling through the air so quickly, tumbling head over heels, and seeing sky, land, sky, and land in a terrifying rotation. The ground was flying up toward him. He covered his face with his hands, and everything went black.

He heard musical notes in the distance.

WEDNESDAY

Nick woke up in a daze. He was still hearing the music from his dream. His phone was ringing. It was Kat. "You are never, ever, in a million years going to guess who were members of the Sisters of Mercy motorcycle gang," she said.

"Kayla and Jordan."

"How did you guess?" Kat sounded disappointed.

"I talked to Ben Sherman yesterday, aka Special Agent Ben Shapiro."

"What did he say?"

"You know what? I'm going to just come over."

"What happened to house arrest?" Kat asked.

"My dad is at the garage, and hopefully I won't run into Tucker or another felony in progress from here to your house."

Nick rode through the woods, and it was the first time he had felt anything close to happy in the past few days. He had been cooped up in the house, and he missed riding everyday. The fact that he was going to see Kat also helped to raise his spirits.

He veered off the trail to one of the jumps he and Billy had built in the woods. He accelerated up the ramp and sailed through the air. He landed and found himself grinning under his faceguard.

"Kat?" Nick called, when he walked through the Mackenzies' front door. The station wagon wasn't in the driveway, so he felt free to shout.

"Upstairs!" Kat yelled.

Nick took the stairs two at a time while peeling off his gear. He reached Kat's room and dumped the guards in a pile, then placed the helmet on the floor.

"Took you long enough," Kat said. She was lying on her stomach with her feet hanging off the end of her bed. Her laptop was open in front of her.

"I took a little detour to hit a few jumps."

"I'm jealous," Kat said, rolling onto her side and propping herself up on an elbow. "So? FBI agent says . . . ?"

Nick sat at the end of her bed and told her everything Agent Shapiro had told him.

"Look at this." Kat turned back to her laptop. "I logged on as Billy." She pulled up Jordan's Facebook page, and there they were, the Sisters of Mercy: Jordan, Kayla, Gabrielle, Maya, Anna, and a dozen other smiling girls, arms around one another's shoulders, leaning in toward the camera. Another picture was tagged Jordan Graham and Kayla Taylor—two twelve-year-old girls with their arms draped over each other's shoulders. Their matching plaid skirts and white button-down blouses looking disheveled from play. Jordan's left knee sock had slouched down around her ankle.

"They look so . . ."

"Innocent," Kat finished his thought.

"Yeah." Nick stretched out next to Kat and read through the posts.

"Well, they don't advertise that they hijack truckloads of pharmaceuticals."

"No, I imagine they wouldn't want to do that." Kat rolled her eyes.

"They sound like best friends. Why would any of them kill Jordan and Anna?" Nick asked.

"Look at this part here: 'Sisters 'til the end,'" Kat read from the bottom of the page. "That sounds pretty ominous."

"You think they killed them because they wanted to leave the gang or something?"

"Why not? It happens in gangs all the time." Kat shrugged, scrolling through more pictures of the smiling girls. "I mean, this was no sorority. This girl gang was hijacking trucks and stealing drugs. Kayla shot an FBI agent! Anything is possible."

"I guess so." But Nick wasn't so sure. "I feel like all the pieces are in front of us, and it's still not making any sense." Nick caught sight of Kat's digital clock on the bed stand. It glowed an angry and unforgiving 5:13. "It's getting late. I better get home." He sighed and rolled reluctantly off the bed.

He gathered his gear and bounded down the stairs. But when he stepped out onto the porch and stopped short. Kat collided into his back and Nick stumbled forward. "Nick, what are you . . . ?" Kat stopped midsentence and stared at the two cop cars and the two black SUVs parked outside her house.

The lights on the police cruisers were flashing blue and red. Tucker was standing next to one of the black SUVs with Agent Diaz. Their angry red faces were close together, arguing in hushed voices. Diaz nodded his head up toward the front porch, signaling to Tucker. When Tucker turned around and saw Nick, his face flushed an even darker shade of red.

"You! What did I tell you about staying home and out of trouble?" Tucker stormed up the front steps, poking his finger into Nick's chest. "Why can't you follow simple directions? What are you doing here?"

"I'm visiting my friend. What are you doing here?" Nick asked, looking past Tucker to the three dark-suited agents who were huddling near the second FBI vehicle.

"I'm looking for you!" Tucker took off his sunglasses and rubbed his eyes. The stocky cop looked weary. He exhaled through his flared nostrils. "I went to your house, but you weren't there. We went down to your father's garage, and you weren't there. Your dad told me where I might be able to find you. It's been a goddamned goose chase!"

"What did I do?" Nick asked.

"One of my patrolmen spotted a gold motorcycle on your street about two hours ago. We think it might have been Kayla Taylor, the shooter from Saturday's robbery."

"On my street?" Nick exchanged looks with Kat. "Why would she still be in this area? Why wouldn't she have run?"

"I was hoping you could answer that for me. Why would she come and see you? You and your friends say you were not involved in anyway with Kayla or the Sisters of Mercy, the murders, or the drug heist, but here you are at every turn." Tucker's nostrils flared extra wide, and his bristly mustache shuddered like an angry animal. "Every crime scene, every clue, there's Nicolas Bishop, again! How is it every time I turn around I run into you?" Tucker took a deep breath and leaned in toward Nick.

Agent Diaz cleared his throat. Tucker straightened taller and stepped back. He gave a small nod to Diaz, and the tall FBI agent climbed the three steps, joining them on the front porch. He wore dark sunglasses, but Nick still felt the weight of his stare behind the dark reflective lenses. "Son, Agent Shapiro has voiced his suspicion that you somehow aided Ms. Taylor in some aspect of the robbery."

"I didn't. I swear," Nick started, but Diaz held up his hand to silence him.

"He is not sure how or why, but he believes you are involved." Diaz removed his sunglasses and ran his tongue along his big square white teeth. He made a small sucking noise as he did this, which gave the impression that he could eat Nick for lunch if he wanted to. Nick hoped he didn't want to.

"I barely know Kayla!" Nick said.

Diaz signaled to the other agents. One of them, a tall man with dark hair and dark glasses, climbed the stairs and handed Diaz a manila folder. Agent Diaz opened the folder and pulled out surveillance photos of Nick standing at Kayla's door. In the photos, Kayla was wearing a tube top and low-slung white pants, smiling in the doorway.

"We had a team watching Kayla's apartment after Anna Rael's body was found. We think there could be a power struggle happening within the Sisters of Mercy. If that were the case, she could be looking for new recruits." Diaz tapped the photo with his finger.

"That's not what that is." Nick was feeling a tightness in his chest.

"Listen to me carefully." Agent Diaz sucked at his teeth. His dark eyes never left Nick, and Nick felt the pressure of his stare like a weight pressing on him.

"I am not interested in pursuing any formal charges against you or your friends, if I don't have to. But I want to catch these women. Whatever it takes. That means you are not going to get in my way."

"I am not in your way. I'm not in anybody's

way!" Nick spread his arms to show that he was just a kid, and not part of a motorcycle gang or a drug conspiracy. Agent Diaz did not look convinced. He handed the folder back to the agent standing by his side, and the man returned wordlessly to the black SUV.

"I am giving you one more chance. When is the last time you had contact with Kayla Taylor?" Diaz asked.

Nick thought about it. All the days were running together, so he had to work backward through the hurricane of events. "Sunday morning," Nick said finally, "when those pictures were taken."

"The day before the robbery?" Tucker asked. "But you also saw her at the robbery, when she shot Agent Shapiro."

"But she was wearing a motorcycle helmet! We didn't know that the shooter was Kayla until you told Nick afterward," Kat added.

"We had no idea she was involved with anything illegal," Nick said. "We thought she was in danger, because two of her friends had been murdered."

"One of her friends was murdered by Billy Mackenzie." Tucker hiked up his gun belt.

"Billy," Kat said through clenched teeth, "did not kill anyone. And that is all we have been trying to do for the past week and a half—prove that Billy was not involved." Kat took a step toward Tucker. "You find out that Jordan was involved with drugs and a gang, and one member of the gang is killed and another shoots an FBI agent, and you still think that Billy killed her?" she shouted the end of her question.

Nick could see her rage and frustration vibrating

through her body. He grabbed her arm and pulled her back behind him. He thought she might lose it and smack Tucker. As satisfying as that might be to watch, Nick could not handle visiting Kat at the county jail. He held tightly to her forearm, fearing she would pounce if he let go.

"This is not helping me catch Ms. Taylor." Agent Diaz put up his hands, one toward Kat and the other in Tucker's direction. "Mr. Bishop, I do not know whether you are aiding Ms. Taylor in her escape, or if you are in danger because of some prior involvement—"

Nick started to shake his head in protest, but Agent Diaz held up his hand and cut Nick off.

"But believe me"—his voice was low and flat as he continued—"I will find out. Do you understand me?" Diaz raised an eyebrow at Nick. Nick nodded.

"If Ms. Taylor does contact you, threaten you, or send you a goddamn valentine, I want to know about it." He handed Nick a business card with an office and a cell number listed.

Diaz sucked on his teeth again and slid his black sunglasses back on his face. He walked off the porch without another word, and signaled the other agents with a barely perceptible nod. The dark suits piled into the black SUVs, and they left only a cloud of dust in their wake as they sped away. Nick, Kat, and Officer Tucker all stood watching the dust settle.

Tucker muttered under his breath something. Nick thought it sounded like "Arrogant prick."

After a minute, Tucker turned to Nick. He rubbed his eyes and sighed. "Go home, Mr. Bishop. Your father is worried about you." He stepped off the porch, and Nick wasn't sure but he thought he heard Tucker say quietly, "Who knows what you've gotten yourself into." Tucker got into his cruiser and pulled away from the house slowly. Officer Tenely, driving the second police car, followed.

"Why would Kayla stay in this area?" Kat said a few minutes after Tucker was out of sight.

"I don't know. It doesn't make sense," Nick suddenly felt very tired. "I don't feel like going home." He knew he should, but he was sick of Tucker and Kayla and the FBI. He just wanted to be with Kat.

"Of course you can stay." Kat led the way back upstairs and collapsed on her bed. Nick stretched out next to her. She shifted her weight onto one of her elbows and used her opposite hand to tuck a dark lock of hair behind her ear. Nick could smell her cherry-flavored lip gloss, and he found himself staring at Kat's lips. He wanted to kiss her—the idea caught him by surprise.

There was a high-speed whirring in his chest that made him feel dizzy and slightly sick. He wanted to kiss her, but there was an invisible barrier, something that kept him from moving and practically kept him from breathing. *Would Kat ever want to kiss me?*

She had never acted toward him the way girls acted around Billy. She never flipped her hair or hung all over him. And what if he kissed her and she was horrified? How would she react? She was more likely to punch him in the shoulder than she was to melt in his arms. "What?" Kat asked.

Her dark lashes framed the question in her eyes. Their faces were only five or six inches apart, and

Nick felt light-headed. His stomach dropped like he was on a roller coaster. "Nothing," Nick said.

Stupid. Stupid. Stupid. Get a grip. He looked away. He directed his gaze to the other side of the room over at Kat's desk and saw her camera on it, charging. He thought of his dream, Kat smiling and waving. Then he remembered her smiling as she filmed him on the podium the day of Jordan's murder.

"Really, what are you thinking about?" Kat was leaning in toward him, so when he whipped his head around in her direction, his temple collided into her forehead with a *whack*. They both cried out and simultaneously grabbed their heads.

"Wow, that hurts!" Kat said, rolling off the bed to look in the mirror at the bright red spot and quickly rising lump on her forehead.

"I'm so sorry. I didn't expect you there!" Nick felt pain pulse through his right temple. He rubbed it with his fingertips, but it did little to relieve the pain. "Are you all right?"

"I don't know. This is the second time in less than a month that you've knocked me around. I'm starting to think you've got it in for me."

"Kat, I'm really sorry."

"I'll get us some ice." She walked out of the room, rubbing her red forehead.

Smooth. Very smooth, Nick thought. *What just happened? And why was she leaning in so close, anyway?* Nick held his aching head in his hands and told himself to stop thinking. It hurt to think. When he looked up, Kat's camera caught his eye again.

"Do you want a soda?" Kat yelled from downstairs.

"Yeah!" Nick shouted back. "Have you watched the video from last Saturday?"

"What?" Kat's voice was muffed, and Nick heard some cupboards banging in the kitchen below. Nick could hear her bounding up the stairs two at a time, and then she was in the doorway with two bags of ice and two cans of cherry cola.

"What did you say?"

"The video you took last Saturday, have you watched it?" Nick held up the camera.

"No." Kat collapsed on the bed and rested a bag of ice on her head. "But we didn't see anything that day. I only recorded you guys. And we weren't anywhere near the parking lot or the locker rooms."

"I know." Nick sucked in air as he set the bag of ice against his temple. "Let's take a look anyway."

"Sure." Kat sounded doubtful, but she dragged herself up off the bed and plugged the camera into her laptop. She found the video files from the race day and played the first one. On the screen, Tweety was roughing up Nick's hair. There was a lot of noise from the crowd and the racing bike engines in the background.

Kat had zoomed in on them from thirty feet away, and the image shook as she walked closer to where the boys were joking around. Billy appeared on the screen from the left. Kat's voice in the video sounded louder than all the other sounds when she said, "That's a good look for you."

For Nick, it was hard to watch himself on screen and remember that was not his life anymore. Everything was different. He had stumbled over dead bodies, had a crush on a girl gangster, and was on the

FBI's pesky kid list. Billy was in jail. Nick felt as though he were watching himself in a parallel universe.

"It feels like it was a million years ago," Kat said, letting the bag of ice slide off her face into her lap.

On screen, Billy reached toward the camera with a mud-splattered hand. He was smiling. Billy was happy in this other universe, this past reality—and free. Kat's foot kicked up into the frame. The video clip ended.

The second clip started with Tweety, blushing bright red, rolling his eyes, and laughing. Nick was not watching Tweety, though. He was scanning the crowd and the background for a glimpse of something, but he didn't know what.

Kat leaned forward and double-clicked on the third video. Nick, Tweety, and Finn stood on the stage. Nick watched himself wave at Kat and then get sprayed with cherry cola. Tweety and Finn leapt off the podium, and the camera followed them. Kat had zoomed in on Finn pouring soda over Tweety's head, and then zoomed back out as they walked back through the crowd. The video clip ended and Nick sighed, letting his face fall into his hands.

"Nick, what are you hoping to find?" Kat touched his shoulder.

"I don't know." Nick shrugged. "How about Billy walking into the locker room alone. Or Jordan walking toward the parking lot—alone. Someone besides Billy holding a bloody wrench. Is that too much to ask?"

Nick's phone rang. "Shoot. It's my dad." Nick answered and listened to his dad's angry tirade.

"Fine." Nick closed his phone.

"I guess you have to go home now?" Kay asked.

"Yeah, I'm pushing him to his limit."

"I wasn't the only person filming that day. Mrs. Fletcher had a video camera, remember?"

"Tweety's old Sunday school teacher?" Nick asked.

"Yeah. She was mine, too, except she liked me! We'll go over to the Fletcher's first thing tomorrow morning and see if she caught the murder on film."

Kat was smirking.

"I know it's a long shot, Kat! I guess I just have to feel like, I don't know . . ."

"Like you're doing something. Anything." Kat looked down at the floor. "Believe me, I completely understand. Preacher"—Kat pointed at Nick and then herself—"choir. Which is why I'm going with you first thing tomorrow morning."

THURSDAY

Some mornings, when the temperature is just right, lying in bed waking up without an alarm, consciousness rises in small, comfortable increments. Before Nick opened his eyes, the sweet scent of vanilla seemed to be drifting in through the window. Something was hovering at the edge of his mind.

Something not quite right.

Nick bolted upright and looked around his room. Kayla was standing by the open window. A few strands of her golden hair danced across her face with the breeze. Gabby was there too, sitting casually on the floor by the bed with a gun in her lap.

"Morning, Sunshine," Gabby said, standing up.

Nick didn't move. He felt a cold sweat break out on his bare back. His fingers gripping the comforter were icy. Gabby walked over to the edge of the bed and sat down. Kayla didn't move. She was staring intently out the window down to the street.

Nick looked back and forth between the two girls. There was an unspoken tension between them. Nick eyed the gun in Gabby's lap and his heart skipped a beat. He made himself tear his eyes away, and he forced himself to speak.

"The FBI is looking for you," Nick said.

"How *is* Ben?" Gabby curled her lip in contempt.

"Alive."

"Thanks to you." Gabby narrowed her eyes and glared at Nick.

Nick didn't say anything.

Gabby laughed.

"You prevented Kayla from exacting justice. But

I've always known justice doesn't exist in the real world. Not for the little people. Not for Jordan and Anna. Not for your friend Billy. It was within our grasp and you stole it from us."

Nick just stared at her blankly. The gun in her hand was distracting him and preventing him from thinking clearly.

"Justice for what?" Nick finally said. "I think you killed Jordan! You framed Billy!"

"We don't kill our own." Kayla turned away from the window. "She was one of us. A sister. Don't you get it?"

"You're not too bright, huh? Have you been listening to what we're saying?" Gabby rolled her eyes. "We did not kill anyone. Kayla shot Ben, because she had to. She shot him because we found out what he was doing."

"You found out he was an FBI agent?" Nick asked.

"We didn't know he was a Fed until we saw it in the papers. We found out he was the one who killed Jordan and Anna," Gabby said flatly.

"He couldn't…. I mean, why would he?" Nick swallowed. He tried to wrap his head around what was happening, but it felt a bit like spiral, like riding the teacups as a kid. Spinning within spinning.

Why were they here? What were they talking about?

Kayla motioned to Gabby. "Show him the text." Gabby kept the gun in her hand, but moved it to her side as she leaned forward and pulled her phone from her back pocket.

"The day Anna was killed, she sent me a text."

Gabby found the text and then showed the screen to Nick.

BS DBLXS US 4 EG. RUN!

"BS—Ben Sherman—double-crosses us for EG. Run!" Gabby translated. "That's how we know. Anna told us!"

"The last thing she did, probably." Kayla's voice was softer than usual. When she turned back to Nick, her eyes were flooded with tears.

"And EG?" Nick asked. "What's that?"

"EG is El Gallo. That's my contact for the drop off." Kayla exhaled heavily and blinked back her tears.

Nick dug through his brain searching for something he had learned in first year Spanish.

"The Rooster?"

Kayla nodded at Nick's translation.

"He's the guy we deliver the stolen trucks to."

"He's our employer." Gabby's voice was full of acid and contempt. "But it's not the kind of job you can quit. And when you get fired, it's with a gun."

"So you thought Ben was going to eliminate the Sisters of Mercy after the heist?" Nick asked.

"We know he was!" Gabby's face was flushed red with rage.

"I should have listened to Jordan when she warned me about Ben," Kayla said softly. "She knew. She had a bad feeling about him, and I should have listened to her."

"I said the same thing!" Gabby snapped. "You can only trust your true sisters, nobody else."

Nick's mind was racing a million miles an hour trying to figure out how to get out of this situation alive. If he could keep them talking, maybe he could find a way.

"What did she suspect him of?" He asked.

"She just had a feeling," Gabby said. "An instinct that he wasn't quite right."

"His timing was too perfect. He showed up just at the right time, with just the right connections to help us with the hijacking." Kayla looked miserable.

"I thought Jordan was being paranoid. We asked around about him, but he checked out. People vouched for him." Gabby shook her head. "But the whole thing was a setup."

"I was so stupid," Kayla said softly. "I thought he loved me. When Jordan was killed, we truly thought Billy had killed her. She did tell Gabby that she was planning on breaking up with Billy. But when Anna turned up dead too? No. No way. What am I, stupid?" A tear rolled down her face and she swiped at it.

"I *was* stupid," she whispered.

Nick watched her. He wanted to believe her, but how could he?

"Ben is an undercover FBI agent investigating your gang! Why would he kill suspects instead of arresting them?" Nick asked in disbelief.

"Don't be so naïve!" Gabby rolled her eyes. "Ben is a dirty fed on El Gallo's payroll. He must have told El Gallo the FBI was tracking the Sisters of Mercy and convinced him to make a sacrifice of us. It's better business for the both of them if we are dead and gone. Silent as the grave, is the expression." Gabby smiled a tight, unhappy smile.

"If the Sisters of Mercy were arrested by the Feds and we testified against El Gallo, he in turn would expose Ben, the federal agent he's got in his pocket. And Ben is the one who would be really screwed. Ben had to protect himself by eliminating the Sisters of Mercy," Kayla added.

"If what you're saying is true, what can I possibly do to help?" Nick asked, not wanting to hear the answer.

"We haven't made the delivery yet. Which gives us leverage in all directions. El Gallo still wants the delivery to go though. This shit is big money," Gabby said. "He thinks we'll make the drop and still get him his cut, but we're going to take that money and get out of town."

"Where are the drugs now?"

Kayla shook her head.

"That's not any of your concern at the moment."

"And why should I help you?"

Gabby cocked her head at Nick. She looked slightly surprised.

"Mainly, so we don't kill you."

A wry smirk returned to Gabby's face.

"But secondly, so we don't kill your father or your little girlfriend first."

Gabby leaned into Nick and ran her gun gently down his cheek. His mouth went dry. He gripped the sheet tighter and felt his pulse pound in his fingertips.

Please. Please. He couldn't speak, but he was screaming in his head. *Just leave them alone.*

Kayla stepped over and laid her hand gently on Gabby's shoulder. "Easy—remember?" The girls exchanged a look.

"And finally, you'll help us because we have hard proof that your friend Billy didn't kill Jordan." Gabby sat back, relaxing a bit, but she still held the gun pointing in Nick's direction.

"You help us, we'll help you." Her eyes were steely cold. "Let's be very clear. We are fighting for our lives here, and we have nothing to lose."

Gabby's jaw was set. She looked fierce and vengeful. Kayla nodded.

"Now, why don't you get dressed so we can discuss the plan?"

"Cute underwear." Gabby was leaning against the dresser watching Nick pull on a pair of jeans. The gun was in her right hand, resting casually on her hip.

Nick was somewhere between embarrassed and angry, but it's pretty amazing how a gun in the room boils down every other emotion and distills it into fear. He buttoned his jeans and walked over to where Gabby stood in front of the dresser.

"You have really nice eyes. Do you know that?" Gabby was looking at him closely.

"I need a T-shirt and socks."

Nick motioned to the dresser Gabby was leaning on.

She tilted her head at him but didn't move.

"Gabby, knock it off. We don't have time to waste," Kayla said sharply.

"You'll grow a few inches, fill out a little, then you'll be a real lady-killer," Gabby continued.

The word "killer" hung in the air. Nick kept his face blank and stared at the gun in Gabby's hand.

Nick was having a hard time thinking straight. He just wanted her and her gun out of his room and out of his life. Nick looked past Gabby into the mirror over the dresser. The marks along his ribs had faded to a yellowish-green. His fat lip had deflated. And the abrasions along his left cheek were now only a crisscross pattern of thin scabs.

Gabby sighed and stepped away.

"What kind of evidence do you have to prove Billy's innocence?" Nick pulled open the drawer and grabbed two socks.

She wagged her finger at him.

"When we have our money, we'll give you all the proof you need."

Nick turned to look at Kayla, but Kayla looked away. She walked over to the window and carefully pulled aside the curtain checking the street side view.

Nick pulled a clean T-shirt on over his head.

"Hey, Gabby, why don't you let him get dressed. Go bring the bike from around the back of the garage. We'll meet you outside in a minute."

Gabby glared at Kayla but walked over to her and held the gun out in her open palm.

"Don't let him get away."

Kayla took the gun, and Gabby stalked out of the room.

"That girl is scary," Nick said after he heard the back door slam closed.

Kayla scowled. "You don't know her. You don't know anything about her or her life."

"Sorry, I just mean"—Nick struggled to find the right words—"well, she's so different from you. You seem, I don't know, not like the leader of a criminal enterprise. Jordan too. She seemed like a regular girl. How did she end up in a gang?"

"Jordan was a runaway. But she never saw anything too rough. I knew her from when we were little. We grew up in the same neighborhood—went to the same school. We got her before she fell in with something bad."

"Joining a gang isn't something bad?" Nicked asked.

"See?" Kayla exploded. "You don't know anything!"

She stepped toward him and jammed her finger in

his chest. She was yelling in his face.

"You can say something like that from your safe, perfect little life, because you don't know!"

"Well, explain it to me. Why do you do this?" Nick really wanted to know. Kayla was smart and young. She could do anything she wanted.

Couldn't she?

Kayla stepped back.

"Why?" She shook her head. "There are a million reasons. Each one of the Sisters of Mercy has her own. But it comes down to one reason, the same exact reason for each of us: we had to. There was no better choice."

"For girls like me or Gabby or Jordan, for whatever reason, we're on our own, and there are so many shades of bad out there. Dead in an alley isn't even the worst of them. Whether you can believe it or not, being part of the Sisters is the best any of us could have hoped for. At least we have one another. And we're not strung out, whoring, getting beat on by some pimp who controls our lives. We control our own lives."

Kayla turned away toward the window and lowered her voice. Nick had to strain to hear her words.

"Gabby—Gabriella—was traded by her mother for drugs. Traded by her own mother! She was thirteen. She's lived a nightmare, but she's tough. She's a survivor. I had my own bullshit family problems, but I was at least a little luckier than her. I was just starting some motorcycle transport back in Phoenix when we met. We started the Sisters of Mercy together."

She turned back to Nick.

"We started small, little courier jobs, but we got better and bigger. We started getting more highway escort jobs. We didn't have to carry guns or drugs on us. We distracted the cops if needed, and the worst me or my girls ever got were traffic tickets. We actually started making some money. We are good at what we do, and I thought that would keep us safe."

Kayla shook her head.

"But something went wrong. Something changed, but I just don't know what."

She let out a sigh of disgust.

"We are all just trying to survive—any way we can."

"Jordan had dreams of more than just surviving," Nick said.

"Yeah, I know." Kayla looked down at the floor. "She was dreaming of some gig in the music scene— like that was ever going to happen."

"She thought she could make it. And go to Africa," Nick said.

"And look where it got her." Kayla's voice was flat. *Hopeless.*

Musical notes rang out. Nick's cell phone was ringing.

Kayla cleared her throat.

"Answer it. It's time to rally the troops. Tell your friends to meet you on the east side of the quarry."

Nick stood frozen with the phone in his hand, listening to the musical ringtone. It was the one he had picked out for Kat.

"I said, answer it." Kayla raised her gun and pointed it at him.

"She doesn't need to be involved!"

Nick's insides felt like they were turning to liquid.

"Don't be ridiculous, you're all involved! If you weren't involved, Ben Shapiro would be dead, and me and my sisters wouldn't be on his hit list," Kayla said.

Kayla cocked the gun and spoke in a cool, cruel voice.

"Answer it."

Nick flipped open his phone.

"Hey, are we going or what?" Kat asked.

Nick swallowed, but he couldn't speak.

"What? Did I wake you up or something?" Kat laughed.

"No. No." He choked on the words. Nick looked at the end of the gun and swallowed hard. "Change of plans."

Nick wiped his sweaty palm on his jeans. He felt like a caged animal. His heart was pounding and his head was filled with the sloshing sound of blood rushing through his veins. Kayla made a "move it along" gesture with her free hand. He only had a few seconds to make up his mind.

"Kat, listen . . . call Tweety and Finn have them meet us on the east side of the quarry."

"What time?"

"Thirty minutes," Nick said.

Kayla nodded her approval.

"Okay, see you there," Kat said, and hung up.

Nick felt sick to his stomach. He snapped his phone closed. This was it. There was no going back. He was leading his friends into danger with Billy's freedom dangling in the balance—all based on Kayla's word.

"Good boy," Kayla said, and lowered her gun. She took her phone out of her back pocket and held down a key.

"Hey, girl," she said. "We're on. They should be there in thirty minutes. We'll be there in ten."

Nick hoped he was doing the right thing. Outside, he kick-started his bike. Gabby got on behind him. He was wracking his brain for a spot on the trail he could maybe crash or throw her off the back of the bike. *Is there any spot bumpy enough to shake her loose?*

"I see your gears turning!" Gabby shouted over the engine noise. "Just get us there, or I swear, someone will get hurt."

She emphasized her words with a dig in Nick's back with the end of her gun. As if he could forget she had it. Nick had never felt so trapped in his life. Kayla got on her GS and led the way down the trail.

If this was the only way to prove Billy was innocent, then Kat, Tweety, and Finn would want to be involved. But it was a gamble. Kayla and Gabby were dangerous—he knew that now. He rode into the woods feeling like he would be crushed by the doubt and guilt that gripped him. He could barely take in full breaths. It was like a dream where you fall deeper and deeper into a hole in slow motion.

Songbirds trilled. Their calls echoed through the

sunlit forest. Green and gold Aspen leaves shimmered in the breeze against the bright, clear blue sky. It was a cruel joke, Nick thought, for the world to be so beautiful, so calm and perfect, while he was leading his friends into who-knows-what kind of danger.

He thought of them all riding the trail to the quarry. Tweety launching off the jump they built last summer. Tweety could get big air, and he loved to do backflips off that jump. Finn liked to do Supermans, letting his feet go out straight behind him.

The closest we'll ever come to flying, Finn says. And Kat. *Kat.* Nick's stomach lurched. *What have I done?* They rode through the dump stench and into the quarry. Nick tried to focus so he could deal with the situation at hand. If he could only shut the lid on his fear, it would be a little easier.

He pulled up next to Kayla and a parked GS 1200. Both BMWs were filthy, but the gold paint and white wings on the gas tank were visible beneath the splattered mud. Gabby reached over Nick and hit the kill switch. She dismounted and pulled her helmet off. Nick sat on the bike and loosened his chinstrap.

A third GS roared from the trailhead and came to a stop in front of Nick's Honda. A petite, olive-skinned woman took off her helmet and shook out her dark curls. She nodded an affirmative to Kayla.

"We're all set," she said. "The other girls are waiting for us."

"Great. Let's get these bikes out of view." Kayla pointed to a little stone alcove with an outcropping blocking the opening from sight.

"Get off the bike," Gabby said to Nick. Nick did what she said. He took his helmet off and scanned the trailhead, listening as hard as he could for the sounds of motors. Gabby rolled his bike about twenty paces away. She walked back to him, smiling and swaying her hips. Kayla stepped up beside her, all business.

"Here's the way it's going to work. I don't want to scare your friends by being here when they arrive. You are going to explain things to them. We are going to be watching from the woods, so it's best if you not try anything stupid. If we work together, we can all walk away with what we want. No one has to get hurt." Kayla threw Gabby a sharp look.

Nick looked warily back and forth between them.

"What do I say the plan is?"

"Deliver a truckload of drugs in exchange for your friend Billy's freedom," Kayla said.

They started to walk away, but Gabby stopped and turned back.

"Or die. Kayla forgot to emphasize that part." She pulled her gun from her waistband, smiled at Nick, then glared for a moment at Kayla, and disappeared into the forest.

Nick heard the sound of Tweety's approaching Yamaha before he saw the bright yellow of the number plate emerge from the trailhead midjump. Tweety landed and sped toward where Nick was standing. He turned the bike and skidded to a stop inches from Nick's feet. Nick could see Tweety was grinning from ear to ear under his face guard.

"You look like shit, Bishop!" Tweety tore off his helmet. "What happened?"

Nick wished he didn't have to go through with this.

"The Sisters of Mercy came to see me." The Yamaha's engine was still running, so he shouted.

"What?" The smile fell from Tweety's face. He hit the kill switch, and the fading echo bounced off the rock faces. "When?"

"This morning."

"No kidding?"

"I am beyond serious, Tweety."

Engine noises in the distance grew louder, and Kat and Finn rode into the quarry.

How can this ever work? What have I done?

Nick tried to at least look calm and like he knew what he was doing.

"What's the good word?" Kat said as she got off her bike. She propped her bike on the kickstand and loosed her chinstrap. Finn did the same.

"Well . . ." Nick took a deep breath.

He waited until Kat and Finn had pulled off their helmets.

"We may be able to get ahold of evidence that could prove Billy's innocence."

"Really? That's amazing! What evidence?" Kat grabbed Finn's sleeve, shaking it with excitement.

Finn was smiling and Kat started to run toward Nick, kind of bouncing up and down with her arms in the air.

"But"—Nick put his hands out to calm her—"we have to help the Sisters of Mercy to get it."

Kat froze. She stared at Nick as if he had just landed from outer space.

"What kind of help?" Finn asked.

"The kind where we deliver a shipment of stolen drugs for them."

Tweety let out a bark of laughter.

"That hit you took to the head was more serious than I thought," he said, shaking his yellow curls.

"Yeah, he's got residual brain damage!" Kat turned away and held her head in her hand. Then she spun back around and shouted at Nick, "What are you thinking? How does this make sense? The FBI already thinks you're helping Kayla! Now you *are* going to help Kayla?"

She shook her finger at him. Her cast was trembling in the air.

"Is this a competition to see who ends up in prison the fastest?"

Kat spun back away and kicked the ground.

"She's a murderer and a thief! She shot an FBI agent! Remember? How can we trust her?"

The boys stood in silence, not wanting to be the first one to speak. Finally, Nick took a step forward. His voice was soft and apologetic, but the finality of the statement rang clear.

"We don't have a choice."

Kayla, Gabriella, and Maya emerged from the woods, after Nick had fully explained the situation to his friends. The gold jackets and pants the girls wore gleamed in the sun. The three of them were straight-faced, but Nick could see the tension at the corners of their eyes.

"So how does this play out?" Kat asked.

"El Gallo has no idea that we know Shapiro is dirty. We told him we delayed delivery to prevent the Feds from discovering where it was going." Kayla's lip curled up in distain as she spoke.

"But we figure, the drop could be a setup to deliver us to Shapiro," Gabby chimed in.

"And we are not about to walk into that blindly," Maya said.

"Once we get the money, we are going to disappear." Gabby put her hands on her hips. "Right?"

She looked pointedly at Kayla.

"Gabby doesn't see the need for reprisal," Kayla said, not turning her gaze to Gabby. Instead, she stared straight ahead and spoke to Nick. "I still think the man who murdered our sisters should die with my bullets in his gut."

"Kayla!" Maya was shorter than Kayla. She grabbed Kayla's elbow and yanked it so that Kayla had to turn and look down into Maya's face. "We'll be lucky to get out of this alive."

She let go of Kayla's arm and spoke more tenderly. "Let it go, for now."

Kayla rubbed the spot Maya had just released and seemed to say more to herself than anyone else, "He should pay."

"That's not our priority right now," Maya said.

"We make the delivery, get the money, and then we'll plan from there," Gabby said.

"Yeah, but let's make it through the delivery first." Maya looked again at Kayla.

Kayla stuck out her chin, but then nodded once in surrender.

"That's where you guys come in," Gabby said to Nick.

"You will wait here. We will call to tell you where you are going. When you get there, we'll instruct you on what to do next," Kayla said.

"But we are going to need some assurances to make sure you go through with it. Something to guarantee you don't call the cops or lead the Feds to us," Maya said.

Nick felt his stomach drop. "What kind of assurances?"

"She stays with us." Gabby motioned to Kat.

"No way!"

"No!"

"That is not happening!"

Nick, Finn, and Tweety began their protests in sync.

"It's fine." Kat held her hand out to silence them but didn't turn to meet Nick's eyes.

Gabby rode over on her bike. She tilted her head, gesturing for Kat to get on the bike too. Kat faced Gabby and glowered at her. She marched over to the GS and kicked her leg over the back. Nick watched her pull her helmet on and fasten her chinstrap. Kat was avoiding his eyes.

Gabby, on the other hand, winked at Nick and flipped down her helmet visor—a blank, reflective shield where her face had been. Kayla and Maya pulled up on their bikes and the three gold BMWs tore out of the quarry. Kat turned her head and looked back one time before the woods swallowed her up.

After the echoes of the engines faded, a heavy silence bore down on Nick, Finn, and Tweety as they waited.

Fifteen minutes later, Nick's phone rang. "Yeah?"

"We're in position," Kayla said on the other line. "Your turn."

"Where are we headed?"

"Uncle Al's Awesome RVs," Kayla said.

"The RV dealership? The drugs are in an RV?"

"Yeah, the biggest rig on the lot. It's the huge black one with 'Outlaw' on the side. Pretty genius, huh?"

"Are we supposed to just drive the RV off the lot?" Nick did not think this was genius. "I'm fifteen. I've never even driven a car!"

"You'll be fine. Riding a dirt bike is good preparation."

"For driving a forty-five-foot big rig?"

"And a trailer."

"A trailer?"

"You're going to bring your bikes with you."

"What about Uncle Al?"

"Don't worry. No one is there."

Nick braced himself against his bike.

"This is never going to work!"

"It better, for your friend Kat's sake," Kayla said. She lowered her voice. "I don't want to hurt her, Nick. But Gabby is pretty high-strung right now. Things are tense. If we don't get our money, there's no telling what she'll do."

"Don't hurt Kat! We'll do it. We'll figure it out." If anything happened to her, he would never forgive himself.

"Just stay focused. Call me in fifteen minutes when you get there." Kayla sounded worried.

Nick snapped his phone shut. He opened his mouth to speak, but Tweety shook his head.

"We got it. Let's go." He pulled his helmet over his fluffy yellow curls.

Finn kick-started his Kawasaki. "This is crazy!" he shouted over the engine noise.

"What else can we do?" Nick waved his hand at the trailhead where the Sisters of Mercy had disappeared with Kat. He pulled on his helmet and slammed his foot down on the kick-start lever.

We have to do this. We do this and it's over. Kat will be safe and Billy will be free. The bike roared to life, and Nick revved the engine. Leading the way north out of the quarry, Nick sped along an old logging road that would eventually run along the backside of the RV dealership. When they got on the lot, they cut their engines and looked around.

"No sign of anybody," Finn said.

There were rows and rows of pop-up campers and recreational vehicles of all shapes and sizes. The sides of the three-acre lot were lined with strings of colored triangular flags flapping in the wind.

"There it is," Nick said. They rolled their bikes to the biggest toy-hauler RV on the lot. The Prevost "Outlaw" Legendary Luxury Coach with a Detroit 60 series diesel engine stood like a shining black-and-silver monument to the American road.

"This is like a tour bus for rock stars," Finn said.

"This thing is sweet," Tweety said.

Nick gave them both a dirty look as he rolled his bike up the ramp and into the open trailer attached to the hitch.

"Sorry," Tweety said, "but it really is."

"Those biker chicks must have set the trailer up," Finn pointed. There were three bike stands, all ready to go. Nick rocked the stand back and rolled his front tire into it, catching his foot pegs on the sides. Then he rolled the bike and the stand forward. The front wheel lifted off the ground and the bike was secured. Tweety and Finn did the same with their bikes. They closed up the trailer and walked around the huge expanse of the bus conversion RV.

They opened the door and climbed the steps to the interior. Nick eyed the massive driver's seat and the massive windshield, looking through it to the ground below. Finn was right behind Nick. He looked down too. "I think I'm experiencing vertigo," Finn said.

"This thing is a beast." Nick shook his head.

"Wow," Tweety said, standing next to the driver's seat and staring into the RV's cavernous interior.

And when Nick reached the top of the steps and peered farther inside, he knew what he meant. The RV had white shag carpeting, black walls, and chrome detailing. The concave ceiling was black acrylic with sparkling dots of LED lights arranged into a plastic night sky. Nick spotted the Big Dipper.

The huge vault of the modern silver-and-black interior stretched forty-five feet back and was filled top to bottom, side to side, with white Symultec boxes. Tweety whistled two long low notes. "That's a lot of pills."

"I'd better call Kayla." Nick flipped open his phone and dialed. This was a monster rig, he was dealing with serious criminals, and he was scared. He still had no idea what they were going to do or how they were going to do it.

"Along the Interstate? Are you crazy?" Nick practically shouted into the phone.

"No one is going to suspect an RV of transporting drugs, especially a fancy one like you guys will be driving."

Nick didn't say anything. He just stared ahead of him at the hundreds of boxes of stolen pharmaceuticals.

"So, as I was saying," Kayla continued, "you'll drive thirty miles north on the Interstate and pull over at the Canyon Hills rest area. The buyers will meet you there. Get the money before you hand over the stash."

"Who will be there?" Nick interrupted.

"It could be Ben Shapiro, but most likely it will be another bike gang. El Gallo likes to use motorcycle clubs to escort big shipments. They're flexible and can easily pull attention away from the load."

"El Gallo won't be there?" Nick asked.

"Don't be ridiculous. He doesn't get his hands dirty. Listen, it will be easy. Just make the exchange. Then you bring the money to us and pick up your girlfriend."

Nick gritted his teeth. He swallowed down his rising anger.

"Where will you be?"

"Just call me when you've got the money."

The line went dead, and Nick closed his phone.

"I'll drive," Finn said.

Nick and Tweety cocked their heads at him.

"I'm the oldest and I've at least taken driver's ed," Finn said.

Nick and Tweety looked at each other and shrugged. Finn got behind the wheel and started the engine. The hydraulics hissed as Finn released the brake and the rig started to roll forward.

There was a laminated plastic sheet hanging behind the driver's seat, and Tweety started reading the specs out loud.

"Six-speed transmission, two-stage engine brake, independent suspension system, automatic self-leveling aluminum wheels, six-way ultra leather passenger seat, ten-disc CD player, GPS, AM/FM/CD player with satellite tuner, and digital surround sound system. This thing has everything! Ooh, and two LCD TVs, a dishwasher, a refrigerator, a programmable microwave, 45K BTU diesel-fired hydraulic heat, in-motion low-profile satellite system, and much, much more."

"Tweety, knock it off!" Finn was slowly pulling the huge RV forward to the front of the lot. It was a straight line, but he was still crawling along, driving old-lady slow.

"You sure you don't want me to drive?" Tweety asked.

Finn had beads of sweat on his forehead as he reached the exit of the dealership and made a right-hand turn on to the main road.

"I'm fine," Finn said.

The RV just cleared the entrance, but they heard a high-pitched squealing noise as the trailer scraped along a parked pop-up camper with colored flags hanging off the front of it.

"Keep going!" Tweety shouted as he peered out the side window, waving Finn forward even as sparks flew.

The trailer cleared the camper with a moan of metal.

"Come on, Mr. Driver's Ed, step on it!" Tweety checked out the window to see if anyone had seen what happened, and Finn accelerated. The bus groaned into a higher gear and the hydraulics hissed.

"Isn't there any way we could tell the police or somebody what's going on? Maybe they could help us?" Finn's face was slick with sweat and scrunched up in concentration as he steered the massive vehicle.

"It's up to us. We have to make sure Kat is safe, and make sure El Gallo, or any other kingpin, doesn't get these drugs."

Nick stared at the wall of stolen pharmaceuticals.

"Come on, Tweety, help me move these."

Nick started shifting the boxes to make a narrow path from the front of the rig to where he thought the kitchen was.

"What are we doing?"

But even as he asked the question, Tweety dug in and started moving boxes alongside Nick.

"We are looking for that programmable microwave, and we are looking for some kind of accelerant."

"Are we all set back there?" Finn shouted.

"Almost!" Nick shouted back.

He and Tweety were deep within the cavernous luxury rig. Tweety was pouring windshield wiper fluid down the stacks of cardboard boxes, and Nick was stuffing metal pieces from the stovetop into the microwave.

"We're about six minutes away from the rest area," Finn called out.

"We're moving as fast as we can!"

Tweety came tumbling over the top of a stack of boxes and landed on the floor next to Nick.

"Try and make those look neat again," Nick said. "We want them to look inside here and not think anything looks out of place."

"Do you know what you're doing?" Tweety neatened the boxes.

"I hope so." Nick was holding the owner's manual he had found inside the brand-new microwave in the rig's custom kitchen.

"I've set the microwave to start on high in twenty minutes. That should give us enough time to unload our bikes, get the money, and get out of there."

Nick held down the final button in the sequence.

"The microwaved metal should make sparks, and the windshield wiper fluid inside the microwave should catch fire and cause a small explosion."

"Then all this cardboard lights up, and the drugs are engulfed in flames?" Tweety said.

"That's the idea."

"Do you think it will work?"

"It worked on YouTube." Nick shrugged and

started stacking boxes in front of the microwave.

"YouTube is a cultural treasure." Tweety stood back and admired their work.

"Okay, this is it. We're here!" Finn called out.

Nick and Tweety squeezed through the stacks of boxes and made their way to the front of the RV. Finn pulled the big rig off the Interstate onto the ramp for the rest area.

"Go wide this time, buddy," Tweety said.

Finn took the RV all the way to the left and then swung wide in a sweeping right-hand turn into the parking lot, this time avoiding any collisions. It was late in the afternoon and the summer sun was low in the sky. The parking lot was full of minivans and families getting out of the car to stretch their legs or grab an early dinner on their way to wherever they were going.

"Let's hurry up and off-load the bikes," Nick said, looking around nervously.

They opened the back of the trailer and rolled the bikes out on to the pavement.

"Who do you think we're meeting?" Finn asked.

"That guy could be El Gallo," Tweety said. He tilted his head in the direction of a balding, middle-aged man in black knee socks and sandals.

If they all weren't so nervous and scared out of their minds, they would have howled over that.

They heard them before they saw them. The unmistakable roar of five street bikes screaming down the Interstate. Nick, Finn, and Tweety spun around to watch them turn off the exit and circle the parking lot like a swarm of angry hornets.

"This is it." Tweety pulled on his riding gloves.

"How are we for time, Nick?" Finn asked.

Nick checked his watch.

"Six minutes."

The pack was made up of some of the fastest street-legal motorcycles available. A Suzuki Hyabusa, a Kawasaki Ninja, an MV Augusta, a Honda CBR, and a BMW GS. As they circled the parking lot, mothers ushered their children and husbands back into their cars. Some people watched, but when the bikers flipped their visors up to return the stares, the onlookers turned away, unwilling to meet their steely gazes.

Nick could feel vibrations in his chest from the sound of the powerful engines.

"No sign of Shapiro or the Feds!" Tweety shouted to Nick over the noise. He was looking around the circle of motorcycles.

"Not yet!" Nick shouted back.

The bright green Ninja came toward where they were standing in front of their dirt bikes. The bike looked brand-new, with some custom alterations. There was no chrome at all on the bike. Everything from the exhaust pipe to the brake rotors and chain was matte black.

The rider was wearing a black helmet with an image on the side of a snarling, blank-eyed pit bull pulling at its chain. He stopped a couple feet in front of them and pulled off his helmet. His shiny black hair was cropped tightly around his head. He wore three small silver hoops in his left ear. A tattoo peeked out of the collar of his black leather jacket. Nick thought it looked like scales, maybe a lizard or a snake.

Nick tried to stay calm. He didn't know what was going on or what was going to happen, but he had the distinct feeling it was best not to talk first. The biker with the neck tattoo was looking at all three of them, but after a few seconds he settled his gaze on Nick. Nick tried to *feel* bigger.

"Where are the *cholas*?" the biker asked. His Mexican accent was absent until he pronounced the last word. Nick had no idea what the word meant.

Thanks a lot, freshman Spanish.

"The stuff is in the RV," Nick said.

"No, *huero*, the Sisters of Mercy—where are they?"

"They couldn't be here. They sent us instead," Nick told him.

"Why did they send you?" The biker snorted a laugh at the three dirt bikes lined up behind Nick. "Why didn't they come themselves?"

He stared unblinking at Nick.

"Were they scared?" the biker sneered.

"Do they have reason to be?" Nick asked.

"Not from us."

Nick nodded once and tried not to think about the explosion that was going to happen any minute now.

I wish they would just get this over with, Nick thought.

The silver GS pulled up next to the Ninja. The first biker rolled back slightly as a gesture of respect, and Nick realized this was the real gang leader. The rider wore black leathers and a black helmet, and when he flipped open his visor he revealed light brown skin and ice blue eyes.

"Check the stuff," he said.

The first biker got off his bike and stepped into the RV. He came out a couple seconds later and nodded at the GS rider.

"Do it." His strange pale eyes did not waver from Nick.

The first rider rolled his Ninja to the trailer and disappeared up the ramp.

"Keys," the leader barked at Nick, holding out his right hand.

"Money," Nick replied, not moving a muscle.

The leader held his gaze. Nick just stared back. He tried very hard to take long, even breaths. Time seemed to slow. The seconds drew out over forever and a day. Then the biker made an almost imperceptible nod.

The red MV circled around the rest of the pack and pulled up next to the GS. The rider pulled his black leather tank bag off his bike and threw it at Nick. Nick caught it and unzipped the zipper just enough to see it was stuffed with $100 bills. He rezipped the bag and snapped the magnetic flaps down onto the sides of his tank. The MV Augusta did a big squealing burnout as the rider pulled away.

The smell of burned rubber filled the air. The leader again put out his open hand. Nick tossed him the keys to the RV. The biker never turned his chilly blue eyes from Nick's, but effortlessly snatched the keys from midair. The leader tossed the keys to the man with the neck tattoo and signaled to the rest of the pack.

The RV pulled out of the rest area parking lot flanked by motorcycles. The leader didn't move or break his stare with Nick until the last of the bikes had pulled onto the highway.

"Tell those girls we don't do business with replacements. If they are a no-show ever again, there will be consequences." He snapped shut his black reflective visor and tore out of the parking lot.

"Holy shit!" Tweety started laughing. "Bishop, you've got balls of steel."

Nick felt his knees go weak now that it was over.

"Seriously, I almost peed my pants." Tweety was shaking his head with disbelief.

"How much time do we have left?" Finn asked.

Nick checked his watch.

"The microwave should be coming on right now," Nick said looking out toward the Interstate.

The RV and the motorcycle gang had already gone about a half mile. The "Outlaw" and its escorts crested a hill in the middle distance. Nick had a sinking feeling that his amateur sabotage attempt had failed, but then there was a flash of light in the charcoal sky and an explosion echoed through the night. Smoke started rising from the point where the RV had just disappeared from sight. Nick almost cheered, until he spotted the motorcycles coming the wrong way on the Interstate, charging through the cloud of smoke.

"Go! Go!" Nick shouted. They all yanked on their helmets, leaving the chinstraps loose and dangling. They jumped on their bikes and took off, heading south on the highway.

Nick was afraid to look back. This had not been a part of the plan. It was stupid on his part. He hadn't played out the scenario to its obvious conclusion. You blow up somebody's drugs, they are going to come after you.

"Stupid! Stupid! Holy shit! So stupid!" Nick was mumbling over and over under his breath.

Tweety was leading Finn and Nick in and out of

the lines of traffic. They were weaving their bikes around the slower-moving vehicles. Their little bikes were nimble, and they could maneuver around the many cars and trucks on the crowded highway more easily than the bigger, heavier bikes that were pursuing them. But as they sped farther south, they emerged from the congestion of rush-hour traffic.

Nick held open his throttle, but the Honda's 150cc engine was maxed out, and the street bikes were quickly gaining ground on the open highway. The MV Augusta came right up behind Nick and bumped his tire. Nick swerved right and then left, trying to shake the bigger bike from his tail. If they stayed on the Interstate, the larger, more powerful street bikes would just run them into the ground.

We've got to get off the main road, Nick thought.

There were houses to the left. Backyards with aboveground pools backed up against the Interstate. Nick pulled ahead of Finn and Tweety and then veered off the shoulder into one of the yards.

Nick gave a quick glance back and Tweety and Finn were right behind him. Out of the corner of his eye he saw the MV, the silver GS, and the orange Hyabusa follow them into the grass. Nick went right around the house and the street bikes went left.

Nick sped ahead, dodging a swing set in the side yard.

Oh, no!

He braked hard and threw down his handlebars to the left as hard as he could to avoid crashing into the white picket fence blocking his way. He yanked his handlebars the other way and made a quick right through the lattice-covered arbor leading to the street.

Tweety and Finn followed his path.

Nick accelerated down the residential street and checked over his shoulder in time to see an orange blur as the Hyabusa crashed through the other side of the white picket fence. The MV and the GS plowed through the wreckage and came screaming after them.

Nick had no idea where he was. There were a bunch of little developments close to the highway, but Nick had no idea where they ended. They didn't have a chance of losing these bigger bikes unless they could find their way to the woods and some dirt trails.

Nick pulled alongside Tweety and shouted, "We've got to split up!"

Tweety immediately veered off to the left and tore down a different street.

"Go! Go!" Nick shouted to Finn.

Finn veered right at the next street.

The MV and the GS were flanking Nick. The MV rider reached over and tried to snatch the bag off Nick's bike. Nick braked hard and slammed down the shifter, letting the two bikes go past him. Then he peeled off down a side street.

The street dead-ended. Nick didn't even slow down as he blew through the cul-de-sac. He jumped the curb and drove through somebody's lawn, hoping it opened up into the woods.

A man standing on his deck next to his grill was stunned as Nick tore up his grass, making a sweeping left-hand turn to avoid the wet sheets on the clothesline.

"My damned lawn!" the man shouted after Nick. "I'm calling the police!"

Nick headed for a line of trees and brush, but they

were just a thin stand. When he came out the other side, he was back on a small residential street. It was getting dark and harder to see in the gray of twilight.

If I just keep heading south and east, I'll run into someplace I know.

The road ended in a T and Nick stopped at the stop sign. He checked left. Nick could see the red and blue lights of an approaching police car. He looked right and the silver GS 1200 was stopped in the middle of the road 200 yards away. The BMW's tires squealed as he raced toward Nick.

Nick gunned it as fast as he could to the left and headed straight toward the flashing lights. He was on a collision course with the cop car. At the last possible minute, Nick braked hard and turned right, missing a duck-shaped mailbox with rotating wings by a few inches. Nick rode up the front walkway and through a flower garden to get to the backyard. Finally, he found the woods. He switched on his headlight and powered through an opening in the trees.

Nick weaved his way through the woods.

I think south is this direction.

But he didn't know for sure. It was hard to get his bearings. His headlight illuminated only about fifteen feet ahead of him, so until he found a trail, he had to crawl along painfully slow. He had time to worry about Finn and Tweety. He wondered if they had been grabbed by the cops or, worse, by one of the bikers. He thought about Kat.

What if the Sisters of Mercy already know we blew up the drugs? And they get antsy about us not being there with the money yet? Would they really hurt Kat?

He knew in his gut they would, but he couldn't even think about it. He slammed that door closed. Nick stopped the bike, shifted into neutral, and fished his phone out of his pocket. *No service. Of course!*

He put his phone back in his pocket and continued to pick his way through the woods. He didn't recognize anything he had seen so far. Just when his frustration was reaching a boiling point, Nick spotted the well-packed dirt of a trail he recognized. *Finally.*

Making much better time, Nick headed south. After about ten minutes buzzing down the trail, Nick spotted something out of the corner of his eye. It was a light. *A headlight.*

Nick felt his heart beat faster. He heard the approaching sound of a motor. *The GS.*

Nick accelerated, but the light grew bigger as the bike behind him gained ground.

Shit! One of the bikers tracked me down!

No one would find his body out here. No one

would know what happened. Kat would be waiting, but he'd never show up.

And the Sisters of Mercy would kill her. Panic slapped at him. The bike behind him lit up the woods in his peripheral vision as it gained on him. He looked over his shoulder to see just how close his pursuer was. *Twenty feet!*

Nick turned his eyes back to the trail and saw there was a sharp bend coming up fast. He grabbed his brakes hard, but it was too late. He threw down his handlebars with all his strength, but he couldn't make the turn. The bike low-sided, and Nick skidded to a stop in the dirt.

A bomb went off inside him—disappointment and regret rained down. *It's over.*

The headlight grew closer and the approaching bike rolled to a stop. Nick blinked into the glaring whiteness. The engine cut out.

All that stuff about life flashing in front of your eyes is true. But it was all the things Nick hadn't done, hadn't said. Kat would never know how he felt. He was squeezed with panic. It was pressing all the air from his lungs. He just had to stay alive to tell her.

A silhouetted figure stepped into the beam of light. "The first rule of racing is never look back, buddy."

The figure squatted down next to Nick.

"Tweety!" Nick couldn't believe it. He didn't know whether to hug his friend or punch him in the mouth for scaring the crap out of him.

"What's wrong with you?" Tweety said yanking Nick up by the arm. "Why did you take off like that?"

"I thought you were that silver GS."

"Did I sound like a GS?"

"I'm a little freaked out, okay? I'm not exactly thinking clearly. Can you give me a break?" Nick slapped Tweety on the back. "Shit, I'm glad it's you! We have to get this money to Kayla and get Kat back!" He was practically shouting.

"Fair enough. Let's just simmer down, though."

Tweety lifted up Nick's bike and rolled it into the beam from his headlight. He checked the bike for damage.

"I'm glad its you too. I wasn't sure I was going to find my way back," Tweety said. "It got so dark so fast once I found the woods. Then I remembered my phone has a compass."

Tweety pulled his phone out of his pocket. "See? But the thing only works when you have cell service!"

Tweety laughed. "I mean, is that stupid or what? Most likely the only time you're going to need a compass is when you are out in the middle of nowhere with no cell service."

Nick shook his head. *Unbelievable—only Tweety could make jokes at a time like this.*

"How's it look?" Nick nodded at his bike.

"No damage, my friend." Tweety slapped the tank a couple times with his hand. "Your shifter is fine. No bent levers. You're good to go."

Nick took his bike from Tweety.

"I know where we are," Nick said. "If we head down this trail another quarter mile or so, we'll enter the quarry from the north end."

"Then let's go. Let's find Finn and go get Kat."

They rode into the quarry and headed to the east side. As they approached the area where they had met earlier that afternoon, a light flashed on and off.

Finn.

Leave it to Finn to beat them back. They pulled their bikes up along Finn's and turned off their engines.

"What took you guys so long?" Finn asked.

"Don't ask," Nick replied.

"Have you called them yet?" Finn was looking seriously rattled. He was pacing back and forth, wringing his hands.

"Relax. I'm calling now."

Nick dialed Kayla's number and the phone rang and rang and rang. Finally, on the fourth ring she picked up.

"Who is this?" she asked.

"Kayla, it's me. Who did you think it was?"

"Do you have the money?"

"Yeah. Is Kat okay?"

"She's just peachy," Kayla said. "Where are you?"

"The same place you left us this afternoon."

"Are you sure you weren't followed?"

"Positive."

"Perfect. We'll be there in five minutes."

The line went dead. Nick stood there stunned. He was trying to process everything, but he just couldn't. He stared up at the night sky. He couldn't believe it. They'd get Kat. Kayla would hand over evidence to prove Billy's innocence and clear his name.

Is this whole nightmare really over?

Engines echoed in the quarry as the bikes approached. Three headlights glowed in the darkness. Nick shielded his tired eyes.

The bikes rolled to a stop in front of them. The engines cut out, and there was silence. The headlights switched off and there was blackness. Just as Nick's eyes adjusted to the dark, he saw a blur and felt the *thump* of Kat against him. She threw her arms around him and squeezed. Her cast dug into his back.

"Are you all right?" she asked.

"Yeah. You?"

She didn't say anything but he could feel her nod against his chest.

"Spare us," Gabby said.

Kat pulled away and stood with her arms crossed, glaring in the dark at Gabriella.

"Where's our money?"

Nick reached over and took the tank bag off his bike.

"Here—catch."

Nick tossed the bag to Kayla, who was still sitting on her bike. She caught it and opened it. With a pocket Maglite she examined the money.

She nodded and tossed the bag to Maya.

"Holy shit!" Maya started laughing.

"I cannot believe the Mickey Mouse Club pulled that off."

"You act like you didn't expect to see us again alive?" Tweety said.

"Oh, don't say that. Pleasantly surprised, that's all," Maya said. "No sign of Ben?"

"None," Nick said.

"Who was there to meet you?" Gabby asked.

"Five guys on sports bikes," Nick answered.

"The Crowned Kings?" Gabby asked.

"They didn't introduce themselves!" Tweety said.

"The one guy had a tattoo on his neck. The other guy told me to tell you if you were no-shows again there would be consequences."

"I told you!" Gabby sneered at Kayla.

"Knock it off. Let's just get out of here," Maya said.

"Maya's right. The other girls are waiting for us.

"All right, kids, thanks for everything," Gabby said. "But we've got to go."

"Aren't you forgetting about something?" Kat said.

"What?"

"The hard evidence that will prove Billy innocent!"

"Oh, that. Yeah, about that . . . I lied." Gabby smirked.

"You what?" Kat lunged toward Gabby, but Maya stepped in the way and leveled a gun at her head.

"Take it easy, sister," Maya said.

Kat took a step back.

"We needed your help, and we didn't think simply threatening you would work," Maya said.

"There's nothing we can do to help your friend, but we do know Ben Shapiro is the killer," Kayla added.

"We can't believe anything you say," Kat said through gritted teeth.

"Believe what you want," Gabby said.

"Listen, kid, I know this sucks, but if it means anything, I owe you one." Kayla slid her helmet over

218

her head and mounted her bike.

"Let's go." Maya put her gun away and swung her leg over her bike.

The three headlights switched on and the motors roared to life. The Sisters of Mercy tore out of the quarry. As the noise faded, all of Nick's hope was bled dry.

"I've got to get home," Kat said. "My mom will be worried about me."

Her voice sounded as dull and hollow as Nick felt. Nick nodded. Billy had been in jail for almost two weeks, and at that moment Nick lost hope that they were ever going to get him out. They got on their bikes and headed in different directions toward their own houses without saying another word.

Nick just wanted to get home and crawl into bed. He was about a mile away when his bike sputtered and stalled out.

Really? Is this really happening?

He tried the kick-start lever. The engine sputtered but wouldn't start. He shook his bike, but he didn't hear any liquid sloshing around in the tank.

Out of gas.

"You stupid . . . !" Nick threw the bike down on the ground and kicked the tire.

He was yelling at himself, of course.

Stupid! Stupid! Stupid!

He slumped down on the ground next to his bike and felt used up. He had been used. Gabby and Kayla had lied to him.

Of course!

Everything they had done that night had been for nothing.

As usual.

Billy was still in jail, and Nick had failed in every attempt to help him.

Useless!

Nick was working up a violent mental assault of himself. He was on a roll. He was getting ready to relive every stupid thing he had ever said and done, every regret, every mistake he had ever made, when Tweety's image flashed in his head—Tweety, that night and other times. Nick wondered how he never let anything get him down—not for long, anyway.

"The first rule of racing: never look back," Tweety had said.

Nick wondered if Tweety, without even knowing it, lived by the first rule of racing. Thinking about it, Nick laughed. He had a mental image of Tweety sitting cross-legged in front of a crowd, giving advice like some kind of spiritual guru.

"Live life like you're riding a race, man," Nick imagined Tweety saying. "Take one turn at a time. Ride hard. Brake hard. Never look back."

Nick laughed out loud, alone in the dark.

I'm losing my mind, Nick thought. But he felt a little better. Despite today's disaster, they had to move forward and keep trying to help Billy. He hauled his bike up and rolled it along the trail toward home.

As he approached his backyard, Nick heard radio fuzz and voices. He leaned his bike against a tree and left it in the woods while he crept forward as quietly as he could. He scoped out the backyard and there were two dark-suited FBI guys walking away from him toward the house. Their flashlights bobbed up and down along the grass. When they reached the house, Nick snuck along the far side of the garage.

He could hear the voices more clearly now. It was his father and Officer Tucker and Special Agent Ben Shapiro.

"I told you, I don't know where he is!" Randy

Bishop shouted.

"If I find out that you are lying to me, I will arrest you for hindering a federal investigation. And believe me when I say, you do not want to spend time in federal prison."

"I told you. . . ." This time, Randy Bishop's voice was more desperate than indignant.

Nick crept closer in the shadows. All the lights inside the house were glowing brightly. He could see into the kitchen through the screen door. His dad was at the table. His shoulders were slumped forward and his elbows rested on his knees. Ben was yelling all kinds of threats, from investigating his finances to shutting down his garage.

Tucker appeared in the doorway. Nick dodged behind a tree, but he was sure Tucker had seen him.

Shit! Nick wasn't ready to talk to the police. He wasn't sure who to tell what. Was Ben a dirty Fed and a murderer, or did Kayla lie about that like she lied about everything else? He needed to think. Just then, the two Feds started walking back toward the woods again. Nick scooted to the far side of the tree to stay out of their flashlight beam.

"Agent Shapiro!" Tucker's voice thundered from inside the house.

Nick's heart stopped. He held his breath.

"Enough of this! The boy is not here. Randy doesn't know where the kid is. You've got some gall to threaten somebody with extortion. That is not official FBI protocol, I imagine? But the papers eat up that sort of thing."

Nick peeked around the tree. Through the kitchen window he could see Tucker and Ben standing toe to toe. Tucker was puffed up with his fists clenched. Ben was much taller, of course, but he was pale and hunched over a bit because of his gunshot wound. He was looking weak and sickly, and Nick was surprised he was out of the hospital and back on the case so soon.

"Are *you* threatening me?" Ben asked.

"Why don't you and your men call it a night? We can ask all these same questions tomorrow morning and it won't make a bit of difference to the case. And you can maybe get some rest, Special Agent. You're not looking so good."

Ben stared down at Tucker. He held his lip curled in a nasty sneer, but Tucker didn't flinch.

"Fine." Ben stalked over to the back door.

Nick pressed himself flat against the tree.

"Douglas! Rodriguez!" Ben shouted into the dark. "Let's go."

Nick heard the mumbling voices of the agents grow feint as they walked to the front of the house. He listened as car doors slammed and two car engines started. He could hear stones kicked up from the driveway as they pulled away. He heard Officer Tucker telling his dad to go upstairs and get some rest.

Nick exhaled a sigh of relief. He closed his eyes and tried to think clearly. He was so tired, all he wanted to do was sleep. *What am I going to do?*

Nick listened to the quiet of the night. The shadows in the yard were gray and black and navy blue.

"He'll be watching the house," one of the gray shadows said.

Nick practically jumped out of his skin. The flash of a match illuminated Officer Tucker's face as he lit a cigarette.

"I quit, you know." Tucker exhaled as he shook the match out. The smell of smoke and sulfur drifted over to Nick.

"Fifteen years ago."

"How's that going?" Nick asked.

Tucker laughed. "I started again the night you found the body of that second girl." Tucker pulled on the cigarette and the ember glow lit up his face again. He was staring out into the night, but he kept talking.

"I got the feeling we had really stepped in it. Something way over our heads."

Nick nodded in the dark.

"But both those murder cases have been taken over by the FBI, so I guess my instinct was right—way over our heads."

His tone was casual. Nick held his breath, not knowing where this was going.

"Now, there was another vehicle fire on the Interstate tonight," Tucker said.

A sudden breeze whipped through the tree canopy. Sounds of rustling and fluttering crescendoed and then died down.

"Yep, about a half mile north of the Canyon Hills rest area," Tucker continued.

Then he puffed from his cigarette, exhaling slowly.

He knows! He must know. Nick's heart was throbbing in his ears, but he didn't dare move.

"And wouldn't you know it, they found all those stolen pharmaceuticals, stuffed into a recreational vehicle and burned to a crisp."

Nick swallowed hard.

"Was anybody hurt?" Nick asked.

"Not a one."

"Do . . . do they know who's responsible?"

"Witness accounts are all over the place. Some people say there was a motorcycle gang with fifty bikers. Others swear up and down there was a white van driven by a man in a turban, who tossed a bomb out his window." Tucker snorted.

"The FBI is sorting through it all. Not my jurisdiction."

Not his jurisdiction? Does that mean he's not about to haul me off in handcuffs?

Nick dared to hope.

"Are you going to tell me what's going on?" Tucker asked.

"I don't know what's going on," Nick said honestly.

Tucker chewed his lip and studied Nick's face.

"I have some advice for you." Tucker dropped his cigarette in the grass and ground it out with his foot.

"Never start smoking?" Nick asked.

"Sleep somewhere else tonight," Tucker said seriously. "I don't know what's going on, but that Agent Shapiro has a screw loose. He's like a man possessed, chasing after the Sisters of Mercy instead of resting and recuperating. He oversteps the boundaries of the law. Did you hear him threatening your father?"

"Yeah."

"Well, that's not the way a law enforcement officer should act, not in America, anyway! I mean, the FBI shouldn't be the gestapo! Those are tactics used by dictators and secret police."

Tucker took another cigarette out of his pack and swiped a match angrily. The match sparked but didn't light. He swiped again and again and again. Finally, a flame blazed, but the match blew out in the breeze before he could raise it to his cigarette.

"Shit!" Tucker tossed the spent match on the ground. He took a deep breath and exhaled slowly. He opened his pack and stuffed the unlit cigarette back into it.

"Listen, this Shapiro is like a mad dog after those girl bikers. He thinks you know something. Maybe he's just overzealous, but you got to wonder about anybody who can't tell that *your* dad, of all people, is telling the truth."

"Will you tell my dad I'm all right so he doesn't worry?"

"I will." Tucker's tone mellowed. "I'm also telling him to get a lawyer and then make an appointment to go in and talk to Agent Diaz. He's an arrogant prick, but at least he's not crazy. I'd be worried if that Shapiro guy picked you up all by yourself. He seems . . . unrestrained."

"You've never worried about me before," Nick said, more than a little surprised.

"Yeah, well, vandalism is one thing," Tucker sighed, "but this is a whole n'other ball game. This is a man who thinks he can work outside of the system. That's not justice."

"We didn't vandali . . . "

"Yeah, yeah. So I've heard you say," Tucker said, but he was already walking back toward the house.

Nick went into the garage and grabbed a gas can. He filled up his tank, but he didn't start the engine. He rolled the bike back away from the house, just to be safe.

Once he was deep in the woods, Nick turned over the engine and rode toward the Mackenzies' house. When he was close enough, he turned off the bike and pushed it along the trail the last half mile.

He left the bike in the woods and snuck from the backyard to the side of the house. It was almost one in the morning. All the lights were out. He edged around the corner, careful to stay in the shadows, to see if the FBI was watching the house. But no SUVs were lurking in the street.

Nick walked back around the house and stood under Kat's window. He flipped open his phone and dialed. The sound of Kat's phone ringing drifted down from the second-story window.

"Hey."

"Hey," Nick whispered.

"Is everything okay? Your dad called here, like, a million times looking for you." Her voice was sleepy. "Where are you? Why are you whispering?"

"Shh . . . I'm right outside," Nick said, keeping his voice low.

A second later, Nick saw the curtain move in the window, but it was too dark to see Kat's face.

"What's going on?"

"Don't turn on any lights. Ben is looking for me. The FBI is watching my house. They could be watching yours."

"What are we going to do?"

"I don't know." Nick felt like he was going to collapse. He really couldn't think anymore. All the spikes of adrenaline he had experienced in the last seventeen hours had squeezed everything else out of him.

"Go to the back door. I'll be down in a sec."

Kat met him at the back door and let him in. She led him tip toeing through the mudroom and into the kitchen.

"Kat!" Nick whispered and squeezed her arm.

"What?" She spun around, panicked.

"I'm starving!" Nick said, still keeping his voice low.

"Oh, my God," Kat sighed. "You scared me."

"I haven't eaten all day."

Nick was too preoccupied to notice, but with the relief of entering the safety and comfort of the Mackenzies' house he had actual hunger pains. His stomach growled loudly, as if to make its own case.

"Geez!" Kat started laughing. She put her hand over her mouth to muffle the sound. "I guess we better feed that thing."

Kat opened the refrigerator and the soft yellow light lit up her face. She was so beautiful, Nick thought. Her long dark hair hung straight as she leaned into the fridge. She pushed a thick lock behind her ear, examining the contents.

"Ham sandwich?"

"Anything!"

"Ham, cheese, mustard, rye?" She opened everything and moved around deftly in the dark, grabbing a knife from the silverware drawer. Nick sloppily assembled a sandwich. He took a huge bite and groaned. Ham and cheese had never tasted so good.

They sat in the dark at the kitchen table and Kat told Nick about the hiding place where Kayla and the Sisters of Mercy had taken her.

"It's an abandoned mine entrance. I can't believe we've never noticed it. We've ridden by it a million times."

"Where?" Nick asked through a mouthful of food.

"It's about two miles north of the quarry. It's off the main trail and the entrance is blocked by a fallen tree and some brush."

"Do you think they are still there?"

"No. They argued about it the whole time, but by the time you called, the others had convinced Kayla to take the money and leave town."

After the first sandwich, Nick felt more sane, and after the second and third, he felt human again. Nick told Kat about Agent Shapiro and Tucker being at his house. They spoke in hushed voices about everything that had happened that day, the RV, the other motorcycle gang, and Kayla's lies.

"If Ben is dirty. . . ," Nick started.

"We can't believe anything Kayla says." Kat played with the cap of the mustard bottle, twisting it back and forth, open and closed. "Actually, they all freaked me out. It seemed like there was a lot of tension between Kayla and Gabriella. And Gabby definitely had that crazy-eyes look"

Kat shook her head no.

"We have to go back to where we left off. We have to look at the facts minus anything the Sisters of Mercy told us."

"The cops are going to find out what we did tonight, or somebody else is. Either way, we're going to end up in trouble." Nick rubbed his temple, which was starting to ache.

"No way. They literally had a gun to our heads. I'm sure we can't get in trouble for that!"

"And we still come back to the main problem, which is, Billy is still in jail." Nick stood up from the table and put his plate in the sink.

"Well, we go back to where we left off there, too," Kat said in that matter-of-fact way she had. "We start over. We rethink the whole thing. We revisit everything we know."

"Can I sleep first?"

"Yeah, I guess that can be arranged."

Kat led him upstairs. They reached the second-story hallway. She opened the first door on the left.

"You can sleep in Billy's room," Kat whispered.

She was standing inches away from him in the doorway. He was close enough to smell her shampoo, a sweet, fruity kind of scent. It filled his nostrils and clouded his brain. Nick all of a sudden had a squeezing sort of fluttering in his chest. He was compelled to reach out to her, but he was paralyzed.

Kiss her. Just kiss her.

A long moment stretched out, punctuated by his deafening heartbeats.

"So . . . I'll see you in the morning," Kat finally said.

And then she was gone. He closed the door and then rested his head against it.

Second rule of racing, Nick thought. *Don't hesitate.*

Nick kicked off his shoes and collapsed onto the bed. His body was so tired, but his heart was pounding away in his chest. He closed his eyes.

Kat standing in the doorway.

Nick's face flushed hot. He covered his eyes with his hands and was flooded once again with the sick, nervous, intoxicating tingling over his whole body.

This is torture, Nick thought.

Outside, he heard the sound of car doors slamming shut. Nick bolted upright. He slid the window screen open, poked his head out the window, and listened. He heard footsteps on the Mackenzies' driveway.

"Check around back," a voice instructed. Heavy footsteps clunked up the wooden front steps and across the porch.

Two flashlight beams flipped on and started sweeping through the side yard. Nick pulled his head inside and flattened himself against the wall. The screen door squeaked open and there were three forceful knocks at the front door.

"FBI. Open up," the voice commanded.

Ben Shapiro!

Nick thought about Tucker's warning and he began to panic. He didn't want to get Kat into trouble, or her mom. He had to get out of there.

Shit!

This side of the house had no porch. He couldn't climb out the window, unless he wanted to try the twenty-foot jump.

Crap!

He could break an ankle. Or his neck! And even if

he could make the jump, he'd probably be spotted by the two agents patrolling the yard.

Damn!

He pulled on his shoes and started to wrack his brain for a place to hide. He had played hide-and-go-seek about a million times in this house, but there were no hiding places that would fool anyone except a six-year-old. He did not want to be caught by the Feds hiding under a bed!

Shit! Shit! Shit!

The door to the bedroom opened and Kat slipped in. Nick could hear Mrs. Mackenzie's footsteps as she stumbled out of her bedroom and ran down the stairs. Nick and Kat listened as her mom opened the front door.

"What is the matter? Is it Billy? What time is it?"

"Sorry to disturb you, ma'am. I am Special Agent Ben Shapiro with the FBI, and I'm looking for Nick Bishop."

"Is he in trouble?" Mrs. Mackenzie's voice trembled.

"I believe he's in danger."

Shapiro's voice carried up to where Nick and Kat were standing. Kat closed the door gently.

"Kat, I have to get out of here," Nick whispered.

"You don't believe him? That you could be in danger?"

"I don't know who to believe. I just need time to think."

A flashlight beam swept through the window from the side yard below, and Kat and Nick dropped down to crouch on the floor.

"You'll have to climb out the window and pull

yourself up onto the roof."

"Are you kidding?"

"That's how Billy sneaks out."

"Billy is, like, six inches taller than . . ."

Kat put her hand up to cut Nick off, and the muffled voices downstairs got louder.

"I'll distract them downstairs." She squeezed Nick's arm. "Be careful."

Kat slipped back out the door and shouted down the stairs.

"Mom! What is going on?"

Nick tied his shoes, tugging at the laces hard, trying to pull his thoughts together.

Stay cool. Breathe. What's the worst that could happen?

Nick poked his head out the window and looked down into the dark yard below.

Oh, right. I could plummet to my death.

Flashlight beams arched across the backyard, moving away from the house.

Or I could be caught and go to prison.

He felt sick to his stomach.

Don't think, climb, he told himself.

Nick put his right leg out the window. He sat on the sill and ducked his head and shoulders out under the open screen. Gripping the inside trim with both hands, he tucked his right foot under him on the sill and pushed himself to a crouch as he pulled his other leg out the window. Once he had both feet under him, he switched his grip one hand at a time to the outside trim. He stood fully upright, clinging to the outside of Billy's bedroom window.

Nick's heart was pounding in his chest, and

falling to his death was feeling like a real possibility. He reached up with one hand and felt the gutter above him. If he were a little taller, he could reach above the gutter to the roofline, but he needed six more inches to be able to reach. Nick didn't want to put all his weight on the gutter. He worried it would just tear off, and he'd break his back when he landed in the yard below.

The voices inside were getting louder and closer. Nick reached his hand out to the right and felt along the siding. He remembered from when he was younger: Kat's house had shutters. Mr. Mackenzie took them down one summer when he painted the house, and he never put them back up. They were still stacked against the back wall of the Mackenzies' garage.

Nick remembered there were hooks that held the shutters open flat against the house. He reached out in the darkness until his hand found the piece of metal hardware with a flat metal hook on the end. The metal piece stuck out about an inch and half, just enough for a foothold.

The voices were right outside Billy's door now. Any minute, Agent Shapiro would burst through the door or the agents outside would make their way back around this side of the house. There was no time left.

Do or die. Nick thought the expression had never been truer.

Nick scooted all the way to the right on the sill. He grabbed onto the gutter and put the ball of his foot on the shutter-hook hardware. Putting most of his weight on his foothold, he boosted himself up with all his strength.

He leaned onto the roof with his upper body, while his legs dangled out over nothing but the night air. Gripping the rough shingles above him, he swung his left knee up onto the roof. With his three points of contact, he carefully pushed himself up, pulling his right leg up onto the roof.

Below him he heard the door to Billy's room slam open. He crouched and stayed frozen in place.

"I'm not lying!" Kat said.

"Well, where do you think he would be, Kat?" Mrs. Mackenzie wasn't exactly yelling, but her voice was raised and strained. "If Nick is in danger, you have to help these men find him!"

"I don't know where he'd go, Mom!"

"Don't worry, ma'am. We'll find him. We'll leave a man here. We'll search the Foley residence and the Clarks', as well as Mr. Bishop's garage."

"Is it that serious? Is he really in that much danger?" Mrs. Mackenzie asked.

"He has gotten himself involved with a dangerous group of people. The Sisters of Mercy are organized, armed, and ruthless." Shapiro spoke through clenched teeth. "And they are tied to a larger criminal enterprise that is even more dangerous. Believe me, ma'am, it's important we find him before they do."

"Sir?" a second agent said. "We've checked the side yards and the back. There's no sign of him."

"Fine. You and Rodriguez search all the upstairs rooms—closets, hampers, under the beds—everywhere."

Nick crept along the edge of the roof toward the front of the house. It was a short drop from the roofline to the roof of the porch, and Nick lowered himself down. He scrambled to the edge and swung his legs over the side, rolling onto his stomach.

Finding a foothold in the wooden lattice on the side of the porch, Nick climbed halfway down. A flowering vine growing up the lattice grew denser toward the bottom. Leaves rustled and the wood creaked under Nick's weight. He let go and dropped the rest of the way to the ground. He crouched on the grass, listening for footsteps or voices.

Time and silence and darkness stretched out on all sides of him. A noise in the trees made his heart jump into his throat, and he bolted through the front yard. He ran as fast as he could out into the street and away from Kat's house, until he doubled over with a cramp. Breathing heavily and drenched in sweat, Nick leaned up against a tree, hiding in the shadows.

They were searching Kat's house, Tweety's, Finn's, and his dad's garage. Nick had nowhere else to go. He needed to think. And he needed to sleep. He was dead on his feet. His head hurt, and as the adrenaline wore off he felt as though all his energy had been wrung out of him.

He couldn't trust anyone. The Sisters of Mercy told him Ben was the killer, but Kayla and Gabby had lied to him already. They had threatened to kill his father. They had threatened Kat's life. How could he believe anything they say?

Then Nick remembered the abandoned mine—the hideout where the Sisters of Mercy had taken Kat. He had a pretty good idea where it was. Kayla and Gabby had left town. And he didn't have anywhere else to go.

Nick circled around the edge of Kat's neighborhood until he could enter the woods behind her neighbor's house. Shapiro and the other FBI agents were still searching for him. Even from the woods, Nick could see that every light was on at the Mackenzies' house. Nick moved through the shadows, until he was sure he couldn't be seen from Kat's backyard.

Stumbling on rocks and roots in the dark, he finally found his way back to his bike. He couldn't risk starting it. The agents in Kat's house were on alert and might hear the engine noise. He flipped on the headlight, kept the bike in neutral, and pushed it along the trail.

Kat said the hideout was north of the quarry, so Nick headed in that direction. His head was throbbing. He thought about just lying down in the woods, but he worried that Agent Shapiro might start a manhunt for him once it was daylight. And he still didn't know what to think or who to believe or who to trust. If Ben Shapiro was the murderer, what would stop him from killing Nick if he found him alone?

He remembered Anna's cold body, soaked with blood, sprawled out in the woods. A jolt of adrenaline spiked through Nick's body at the thought. All the fatigue drained out of him. Fear flooded his limbs in its place, and he picked up his pace. He kept looking from side to side and behind him. But outside the beam of his headlight, the darkness all around him was complete.

Finally, he reached the edge of the quarry, and he kick-started the bike. The roar of the engine filled the night, second in volume only to the drumming of Nick's heart in his throat and the pounding in his ears. He needed to be focused to ride the trails at night. His hands were shaking, so he closed his eyes and breathed out hard several times. With each exhale, he forced out his fear. With each inhale, it loosened its grip on his chest and he could think, and see, and hear more clearly. Once he had pulled himself together, Nick rode two miles north of the quarry along the main trail, searching for the fallen tree Kat had described.

To the left but parallel to the trail lay a huge felled oak. Its bare branches rose twenty feet in the air and blackberry brambles and honeysuckle vines grew up and around it. Nick pushed his bike around the length of the tree. In the headlight's beam, Nick could see a dark crevasse in the hillside, an opening between two overgrown wild roses. He pushed his bike through the curtain of flowers and thorns and stepped into a long, narrow tunnel.

Wooden supports lined the walls and the low ceiling. Ten feet in, the abandoned mine split into three. Nick shone his headlight down each of the tunnels. The one to the right opened up to a round twelve-foot-by-twelve-foot chamber. There were a lot of footprints and tire prints in the dirt floor.

This is where the Sisters of Mercy held Kat.

The middle tunnel opened up to a smaller chamber, long and narrow, with two sleeping bags laid out on the dirt floor. The third fork was another tunnel. It was only about three feet wide. It curved sharply to the right and disappeared into shadows. Leaned up against the wall were some old tools, a rusty shovel, and a pail.

Nick turned his bike around and guided it backward into the third tunnel, maneuvering the bike past the curve. He leaned the bike against the wall and took off his shirt. He used his shirt to erase the tracks of his bike and his footprints from the entrance, and worked his way back to his bike.

He pulled his bike the rest of the way around the curve so that he and it couldn't be seen from the entrance. The tunnel was musty and cold. Nick shook the dust from his shirt the best he could and put it back on. He flipped off the headlight and sank down to the dirt floor in total darkness.

Hiding in the dirt in the dark, Nick did not feel safe. If he let himself, he could worry about being discovered, or the mine shaft collapsing in on him, or big hairy spiders crawling all over his skin. But whether he held his eyes open or let them fall shut, the velvety darkness around him was the same. So he gave up on his worries and gave in to his exhaustion.

FRIDAY

A voice came to him through a fog. He opened his eyes but saw nothing. He held his hand up, but he couldn't see his fingers an inch from his face. His neck was sore and his body ached.

The voice got louder. Nick could see the bobbing of a flashlight beam bouncing off the far wall of the tunnel, but the light didn't reach all the way back to his hiding spot. He sat still, holding his breath.

"The FBI has roadblocks up on the major roadways, but we can come in and out through the woods."

There was a moment of silence. Nick craned his neck to see out toward the light.

"Yes, sir. I understand. But Kayla has been telling all of us that you wanted us dead. She convinced most of the other girls. They believed her and left town."

She must be talking on the phone with someone.

"I will put this right. That's why I'm back. She's on her way now, and when she gets here, she's dead. I swear. And then I will get the girls ready for the next job."

Another pause.

"You can be sure of that, sir. Kayla isn't the leader of the Sisters of Mercy anymore. I am."

Nick recognized Gabriella's voice echoing around the chamber.

"I said I'd take care of her! Then the Sisters of Mercy will be back to work."

The phone call was over, and Nick strained to hear in the darkness. There was movement in the far chamber, but Nick could only guess what Gabby was doing.

Was she really planning on killing Kayla? Or had she lied to whoever was on the phone? If it was their contact, El Gallo, then Gabby had lied to Kayla about fearing for their lives. Nick's mind raced back to the text message Gabby had shown them. The text message sent from Anna's phone. But what if Gabby sent that text from Anna's phone, after she had already killed her? And if she killed Anna, did she kill Jordan too?

But why? Why would Gabby want her friends dead?

The sound of a motorcycle traveling down the trail carried on the breeze into the mineshaft. Nick sat frozen in place. The engine sound died, and he could hear footsteps approaching. A second flashlight beam bounced off the walls and then disappeared in the far chamber.

I have to do something!

Nick felt weak and his stomach rolled, but he forced himself to his feet. His legs felt shaky as he stood and felt his way along the wall in the dark. He paused when he heard Kayla's voice.

"Gabby? Are you all right? I came back as soon as I got your message. Don't worry, girl, I'll get you out of here."

"You're not going anywhere," Gabby said.

"What are you doing with that?"

"What do people usually do with guns, Kayla?"

"After everything we've been through together! Why?"

"Because even after everything we've been through, you are willing to let it all slip away."

"We have no choice, Gabby! If the Feds don't get us, El Gallo will have us killed. We have to split up to survive. You said so yourself."

Nick flipped open his phone and dialed on the backlit keypad.

Pick up. Please, please pick up!

He held it against his chest and prayed that the girls' shouting would cover any sounds he was making. He held the phone out in front of him, and he followed the wall to the entrance of his hiding spot. With every step, the voices got louder.

"You were willing to throw it all away long before this, Kayla!" Gabbed shouted.

"I was not. Have you gone crazy? What are you talking about?"

"I know you were going to let Jordan walk out on us. I know she wanted to leave the Sisters of Mercy, but that is not the way this works! No one walks away alive. You join, you join for life!"

"You killed her? Gabby? You killed Jordan!"

"I had to. I couldn't just let her walk away."

"That was not your decision to make!"

"I made it my decision."

"Why? Why? She was one of us."

Nick could hear Kayla sobbing. He felt the handle

of the shovel leaned up against the wall and put his phone in his other hand so he could grip the shovel with his right. He continued to feel his way forward, holding the phone out ahead of him.

He heard Kayla's ragged breathing as he stepped closer.

"And Anna? Did you kill her, too?"

"She knew, somehow. I didn't want to kill her, but she wasn't going to keep her mouth shut."

"And the text about El Gallo?"

"That was me," Gabby said.

"But the Fed?"

"That was just lucky. I made all that up and you bought the whole conspiracy theory by the spoonful."

"Lucky?" Kayla's voice was flat. "I almost killed him because of your lies. And this is what you wanted all along. Me dead and out of your way. Why didn't you just kill me to begin with?"

Nick crept past the entrance to the second chamber. He was at the entrance to the large chamber. The two flashlights lit a long narrow line within as the two girls faced each other.

"I needed to win over the rest of the girls. When I meet up with them and tell them El Gallo killed you but will let them live as long as they pledge an oath to me, I think I will win their loyalty. And then the Sisters of Mercy will be a force to be reckoned with."

Nick wanted to run away. His hands were slick with sweat. He set his phone down on the ground. And then he stood frozen.

I don't want to die. I don't want to get shot.

But could he run away and let someone else die? Could he let Kayla be murdered?

"Listen to me, you put us all in danger, Kayla. If anybody can walk in and anybody can walk out whenever they want, you put us all at risk. Jesus, you let this Fed in on our operation! You were always soft!"

The click of the safety made Nick jump. He dove toward the closest beam of light and swung the shovel as hard as he could. The gunshot echoed through the surrounding darkness.

"Is she dead?"

Nick stood in the ring of Kayla's flashlight. Gabriella lay motionless on the ground.

"I don't know." Nick bent down and held his fingers on her neck, under her jaw. He felt Gabriella's warm and steady pulse beneath his fingertips.

"She's alive."

"Well, then I'm gonna kill her!" Kayla stepped forward and grabbed the gun from where it lay on the dirt floor.

"No!" Nick shouted. "Don't kill her." He stepped in front of Gabby, casting a long shadow over her body.

"If you kill her, that's all you'll ever be—a killer." He squinted into the bright light, unable to see Kayla's face. "You're more than that. Jordan would want you to be more than that."

"I can't let her get away with this! She was the one. She murdered Jordan and Anna!"

"I know. She's not going to get away with it." Nick picked up Gabriella's flashlight and searched the ground a few feet away. He picked up his cell phone and showed it to Kayla.

"I recorded her confession." Nick held the phone out in the light, and very deliberately snapped the phone closed, ending the connection. "The FBI could be on their way any minute."

As soon as Agent Diaz checks his voicemail, Nick thought.

Kayla stared at Nick, unmoving.

"You still have time to get out of here." Nick took a step sideways, leaving the exit clear.

Kayla took a step toward Nick. The gun glinted in the beam of his flashlight as she lowered it to her side.

"And do what? Go to Canada to become a singer/songwriter?" She took another step and stood beside him.

"Sure." Nick swallowed. "Why not?"

Kayla leaned in and kissed him on the cheek.

"I can't sing."

She smiled, and then she was gone. The GS motor came to life outside the mine entrance, and Nick listened as the sound of her bike disappeared into the woods.

SATURDAY

"I can't believe, after all the crazy, stupid, dangerous, and illegal things we've done over the last two weeks, that it all worked out!"

"Thanks, I think." Nick was holding his head in his hands, staring at the floor between his knees.

"Lighten up, Bishop. You're a full-fledged hero."

Nick could hear Tweety crunching on something on the other line, handfuls of something from the sound of it.

"I mean"—*crunch, crunch, crunch*—"enjoy it!" *Crunch, crunch, crunch.*

"I still can't get over it all. I can't help feeling like . . . I was so stupid."

Nick starred down at his shoes.

"I wish none of it had happened at all. I mean . . . Billy spent two weeks in jail. Jordan and Anna are still dead."

"Girls are smart, my friend," Tweety said. "Smart. Treacherous." *Crunch, crunch, crunch.* "Devious. Dangerous."

Nick rolled his eyes but didn't say anything.

"Bishop, Gabby lied to everybody. And she was good at it. Even her best friends didn't know what a psycho she was. How could you have known? Seriously, don't take the hero thing too seriously."

Nick listened while Tweety swallowed.

"I hate to tell you this because I know you are going to be very, very disappointed, but the entire universe does not rest on your shoulders." *Crunch, crunch, crunch.*

SUNDAY

FBI Break Up Drug Trafficking Ring
JULY 8 – USA Today – FBI Officials held a press
conference yesterday at a warehouse in Colorado that
was the hub for trafficking drugs and guns throughout
the Southwest. The FBI has a witness in custody who
knows intimately the workings of the alleged ring.
Twenty-five arrests have been made so far.

Michael "El Gallo" Thompson is the alleged
kingpin and mastermind of the illegal operation.

"Mr. Thompson allegedly ran the ring from a
logistical standpoint. We believe he arranged for the
acquisition, the transportation, and the sale of bulk
contraband and drugs. We believe he then hired out
subcontractors, mainly outlaws, to execute each
transaction," said Special Agent Richard Diaz, who
was head of the federal investigation.

According to the FBI, members of the motorcycle
club the Sisters of Mercy have been implicated. Maya
Lincoln, 22 years old, and Kayla Taylor, 19 years old,
and the other surviving members are presently on the
FBIs Most Wanted list.

Musical notes rang from Nick's back pocket. He
put down the paper and answered it. "Hi, Kat."

"Are you reading this?"

"Yeah. Gabby must be their witness."

"So, what—she gets a deal?" Kat sounded
outraged.

"Sure, if she gives state's evidence against El
Gallo. I'm sure they made a deal with her. She'll still
go to jail for murder."

"And what about you guys? I gave my statement to Agent Diaz but haven't heard anything."

"No charges are being pressed against us for the RV fire. We all gave our statements and they decided we were coerced. 'Gun to your head' and all that. And after a couple of hours with Finn and Tweety in an interrogation room, I don't think Diaz or Shapiro ever want to see any of us again."

"I bet," Kat laughed.

"How's Billy?"

"Oh! He is so great! When they brought him home last night I have never seen two people as happy as him and my mom." Kat sounded pretty ecstatic herself. All charges had been dropped, with an apology from the West Central Police Department.

"He's still sleeping, but he'd love to see you later. We're having a bunch of people over for a barbecue next weekend to celebrate."

Nick could hear Mrs. Mackenzie say something in the background.

"Nick, my mom says to make sure your dad comes too."

"Okay. We'll be there."

As soon as Nick hung up his phone rang again.

"Are you looking at the paper?" Tweety asked.

"Well, hello to you too," Nick said.

"Are you?"

"Yes." Nick still had the paper splayed out on the kitchen table in front of him.

"It's the guy!"

"What guy?"

"El Gallo really was the bald guy with black socks in the parking lot!"

"He is not!" Nick looked again at the picture in the paper of Michael Thompson. The man was thin and balding. He looked like an accountant, not a gangster. But he was wearing big dark sunglasses, a dark suit, and a dark trench coat. It was hard to imagine him in socks and sandals.

"It's totally him," Tweety said.

"It is not."

THE FOLLOWING SUNDAY

Mrs. Mackenzie was talking to Nick's father, but she wasn't really paying attention. Her eyes kept drifting over to where Billy sat at the picnic table eating his third hamburger. She was smiling, and she kept tearing up, looking at Billy, nodding as if she were listening. Smiling. Nick knew how she felt.

The Mackenzies' backyard was filled with people. Mr. Clark was manning the grill and Mrs. Clark was prowling around the tables, filling up empty chip bowls, putting dollops of food on people's plates, and picking up empty glasses. Everyone who passed by Billy patted him on the back or mussed his hair. The two girls flanking him were leaning into him, their hands on his knees, their arms around his shoulders and waist.

Mrs. Clark came by the table and everyone guarded their glasses, but Tweety was telling a story and not paying attention. She snatched his empty glass. He bounded up and took his glass back. "Mom! Relax, would you?"

Nick got up from the table and refilled his plate. Standing over by the buffet with Mr. Foley, Mr. Kratchner was eating off his plate standing up. He was looking a bit like Humpty Dumpty with a paper napkin tucked into his collar covering his tie, but not his huge round belly.

"Hi, Mr. Kratchner. Hi, Mr. Foley."

Finn's grandfather nodded.

"Hello, Mr. Bishop." Kratchner smiled, his teeth coated with potato salad. "You're quite the hero in all of this."

"No," Nick said, and he meant it. "I was just in the right spot at the right time. More dumb luck than anything else."

"Nonsense. You have to give yourself credit where credit is due." Kratchner shoveled another forkful of potato salad into his mouth. "Even William says you're the one responsible for proving his innocence."

Finn came up and elbowed Nick in the side. "Yeah, he's just being modest. He's a modern-day Nancy Drew."

"No, really, I'm not being modest—I really sucked at the investigating thing. I made mistakes at every turn. I fell into every trap. I believed people when they lied and I didn't when they told the truth," Nick shuddered. He still felt a weight pressing on his chest. "I made the wrong assumptions. I came to the wrong conclusions."

Nick shrugged. "But Billy is free, and my friends are safe. Nothing else matters."

Mr. Foley swallowed his mouthful of food and looked thoughtfully at Nick.

"Sometimes just our thoughts and intentions bring about change in a situation," Mr. Foley said. "I believe that."

"I have every intention of eating junk food until I puke," Finn said, filling his plate with potato chips.

Mr. Foley rolled his eyes.

"The way to Hell is paved with good intentions. Isn't that what they say?" Mr. Kratchner asked.

"Mmm." Mr. Foley nodded. "Perhaps. One saying goes: You may have a heart of gold, but then so does a hard-boiled egg."

"Ha!" Mr. Kratchner started laughing and Nick stepped away as politely as he could to avoid the hailstorm of food bits flying out of his mouth.

Grown-ups are so weird, Nick thought.

He went into the house and watched the party for a while from the kitchen window. Tweety was now doing some kind of chicken dance, Billy was laughing, and everyone looked . . . happy. But Nick couldn't quite get over the part chance and luck played in their lives—who got away with their crimes and who paid for their crimes more than they owed.

Kat came through the sliding glass doors, carrying an empty platter. "Mr. Kratchner finished off the potato salad!" she said. "That man can eat."

Kat rinsed the platter off in the sink. She dried her hands on a dish towel and then joined Nick at the window. Her cast was finally off, but a ghost of it remained; tan lines marked where it had been across her fingers and a third of the way up her forearm. She was wearing blue shorts and one of her signature slogan T-shirts. This one read I'M HUGE IN JAPAN.

"Come on outside," Kat said.

"No, not yet."

"What, are you hiding in here?" she asked, half joking.

"No. It's just . . . it's so hard to wrap my head around everything that's happened. It almost didn't seem real at the time, and now that it's over, it's hard to believe *this* is real."

"Yeah, I know what you mean," Kat said.

"Your mom seems really happy," Nick said, watching Mrs. Mackenzie in the yard.

"You have no idea. Six more weeks, and my dad

will be home. She is beyond happy."

They watched out the window in silence. Nick knew Kat was in his life for a reason. If the rest of life was all chance and luck, then so be it.

Kat took his hand. "Are you happy?" she asked.

He felt Kat's soft, smooth fingers against his, and sure enough, he was.

I hope you enjoyed *Mud, Blood and Motocross*. The second book in the series, *Crash and Burn*, and third book in series, *Killer Air*, are both available where books are sold.

Help spread the word about this series by leaving a product review on Amazon.com.

For more information, visit **www.mickwade.com**.

An excerpt from *Crash and Burn* by Mick Wade:

Nick Bishop was fourth coming out of turn one. Passing the rider ahead of him, he accelerated down the straightaway with the throttle wide open, hoping to gain a second or two through the whoops. The motor screamed as he kicked the bike into fifth gear. He raced up the first ramp and launched into the air a tire length behind Tweety. Nick scrubbed as low as he dared across the thirty-foot gap.

Tweety took the jump so high, he disappeared from Nick's peripheral vision. A freestyle rider at heart, Tweety was always showing off midair—doing a tail whip midrace and losing valuable time.

Even as Nick flew through the air, he was focused on his landing. He yanked his handlebars up, barely clearing the triple but hitting the dirt a heartbeat before Tweety. Now in third, Nick accelerated toward turn five, chasing down Finn Foley, who was in second. He felt a little tug.

In an instant the bike went out from under him.

Nick was sliding across the track. His legs were thrown off, but he gripped the clutch with all his strength. The gravelly noise his helmet and back pad made as his body was dragged through the dirt filled his ears. Nick sensed rather than saw the other racers flashing by.

Don't hit me! Please don't hit me!

It was all he could think of. His handlebar had buried itself in the dirt as the bike slid to a stop at the edge of the track. Nick felt a spike of pain in his left shoulder, but he still gripped the clutch. He ignored the pain and rolled over toward the bike.

It didn't stall out!

Still holding in the clutch, Nick started digging like mad with his free hand to uncover the front brake lever and the throttle from under six inches of dirt.

Come on! This isn't over!

Time was ticking away. More riders sped past him. He was losing a position every quarter-second he wasted.

Come on!

Steam was pouring out of the radiator from a puncture.

It will make it through the rest of the race, Nick thought. *If I can get back out there.*

Finally, he wrenched the bike free, jumped on, and took off after the rider ahead of him. It was a full-on charge after that. Most of the other racers had passed him while he was down. He would have to battle his way up from the back of the pack.

He opened the throttle and sped like a madman toward turn six. He rode to the far outside corner and hit the brake hard, wrenching the bike into a ninety-degree turn. His back tire slid out and he ripped up the inside of the curve passing three riders at once.

That's it.
Now faster!

Lap after lap, Nick gained and gained. He wasn't thinking about lap times or race lines. He wasn't thinking about championship points. All he was thinking about was eating up the gaps between him and whoever was in front of him.

Catch the next guy.
Now catch the next guy.

That's all that was going through his head. Coming up from behind the pack he had to blast through clouds of dust and clumps of dirt flying off the back tires of the riders he was chasing. He tasted the grit between his teeth.

He had to anticipate what lines the other riders were going to take. He could see farther and farther up the field, and he was choosing his lines without thinking, just trusting his instinct and his timing. He accelerated up the outside of the straightaway and blew by two more riders.

"Okay, that was unbelievable!" Billy Mackenzie slapped Nick hard a few times on the back. Plumes of dust exploded from Nick's shirt with every slap. Nick pulled off his helmet and pushed his sweat-drenched hair off his face.

"From seventeenth to second," Billy added. "Unbelievable!"

"Nice race!"

"Nice riding!"

Nick was getting pats on the back and thumbs-ups from people in the crowd as he pushed his bike past.

"Bishop!" Tweety shouted as he rode up beside them. "I saw you slide out, Bishop! I couldn't believe it! Hangin' on to your clutch for dear life!" He jumped off his bike and put down the kickstand. "I almost crashed, I was laughing so hard."

"Aaaghhhh! Aaaaaghhhh!" Tweety acted as if some unseen force were jerking him by the arm five feet one way and then five feet another way as he imitated Nick's slide across the track.

"You're just jealous!" Billy grabbed Tweety in a headlock and gave him a noogie through his thick mass of curls.

"Yeah, he wouldn't have snuck by you—twice—if you hadn't taken the jumps so high," Finn joined in.

"Yeah, but I looked good!"

Tweety wriggled free and made a show of fixing his hair, which on the best of days looked like a bright yellow clown wig. Today, Tweety's blond 'fro was matted down from his helmet and damp with sweat.

"Hi, Billy!"

"Hi, Billy! We saw you!"

Two girls in supershort jean cutoffs and short tank tops stood by the track fence smiling at Billy. They had matching belly-button piercings. The two silver rings glistened in the sun, drawing attention to the smooth bare skin of their stomachs.

"You were so good!" The shorter one bounced on her toes as she spoke. The other one giggled and waved. Billy handed Nick his helmet with a wink.

"Michaela! Alex! You made it!" Billy swaggered toward the girls, who were cooing and gushing and bouncing as all girls usually do when they're around Billy. The sun glinted off Billy's blond hair and his white plastic chest protector.

He really does look like Captain America, Nick thought. Billy flashed his big smile, and Nick watched as both girls actually swooned a little. Nick shook his head. *Unbelievable.*

He wasn't jealous of Billy. Billy was eighteen, three years older than Nick, and like a brother to him. And it wasn't even like Nick wanted every girl to swoon in his presence. *Although I think I'd survive if they did.*

But Nick was not as tall and muscular as Billy. Billy was a golden boy: blond hair, blue eyes, and girls just flocked to him. Nick had dark hair and dark eyes, and he knew he wasn't ugly—just average.

Maybe a little on the skinny side. He did hope time and the weight bench in his basement would change that eventually, but he wasn't shooting for Mr. Universe or anything. Besides, there was just one girl Nick really cared about. Thinking about her made his stomach flip.

Ignore it, he thought.

Although that was easier said than done, especially when she was there, walking toward him…

260

Made in the USA
Las Vegas, NV
17 September 2021